Montana Cowboy Romance

2020

MONTANA COWBOY ROMANCE

A Wyatt Brothers Romance

JANE PORTER

TULE
PUBLISHING

DEDICATION

Thank you to my amazing first readers:
Sharon
Michelle
Julie
Elisabeth
Judy
Danielle
& Lee

You always give such wonderful feedback. I'm grateful for
your thoughts, and endless support.

Dear Readers,

I'm really excited to share with you, MONTANA COW-
BOY ROMANCE, the first book in my new Wyatt Brothers
series. Rugged rancher Joe Wyatt is done dating and looking
for love, and so, he places an ad for a wife. Sophie Correia, a
farmer's daughter from Central California, answers the ad,
and she is perfect for Joe… until the sparks fly. These two
have chemistry galore, something neither of them expected
or wanted. They are supposed to be entering a practical,
businesslike marriage, not one with emotions and passion.

Hope you will like the tough, sexy Wyatts and their cattle ranch high in the Gallatin Mountains, overlooking
Yellowstone River, in beautiful Paradise Valley as much as I
do. The four Wyatt brothers—Joe, Sam, Billy, and Tommy—grew up participating in junior rodeo, before joining
the Professional Rodeo Cowboy Association. The only thing
they love more than their family is competition.

Stay in touch with me, and let me know what you think
of Joe and Sophie's story. You can find me online, or feel free
to email me anytime, jane@janeporter.com.

Here's to happy-ever-afters!
Jane

CHAPTER ONE

J OE WYATT ROCKED on his heels, trying to stay relaxed as he waited for his soon-to-be bride to enter the terminal. One hundred years ago, he would have been meeting her train in Marietta. Today, he was meeting her plane in Bozeman.

It'd been three months since he'd placed the ad that he was looking for a wife, three months since strangers began answering the ad. Three months where he'd questioned himself even as he explored options, but the questions and doubts were behind him. Sophie had been his first, and final, choice and he, apparently, was hers, as the daughter of California dairy farmers would be stepping through the arrival gate any moment.

He knew what she'd looked like. Medium height, brown eyes, high cheekbones, a strong brow, and dark brown hair. They'd had a half-dozen calls before they had their first FaceTime conversations, and then two more FaceTime conversations after that where they discussed what they wanted, and expected, and how they'd break the news to their families if they really went through with it.

They'd agreed on a simple story. They'd met online—which was true—and they'd become very attached and wanted to be together. Thus, Sophie's arrival today.

What their families wouldn't know was that if Sophie and Joe clicked in person, they were planning on being married at the end of the week. They weren't going to do a long engagement. Sophie was leaving her world behind, and he was determined to include her fully in his.

His granddad and mom knew he'd come to the airport today to meet Sophie's plane. They didn't know much else about her.

But why should they? He didn't know much about her, either.

And then she was there. He spotted her immediately. Sophie Correia looked like a California girl as she walked through the sliding glass doors, wearing jeans, boots, and a cropped denim jacket. It was her waist-length hair that gave her away, hair so dark it looked like coffee in the terminal lighting. She wore a backpack, and pulled a small roller bag, and had polarized sunglasses perched on her small, straight nose.

Her gaze scanned the crowd and, as she impatiently pushed a long strand of dark hair back from her forehead, she reminded him of a California movie star, young, glossy, pretty. Almost too pretty, and he felt a kick of disappointment because he had a sinking suspicion that she'd hate the ranch. The Wyatt ranch was remote, high in the Gallatin mountains, thirty minutes from anything.

He cut through the thinning crowd. "Sophie? I'm Joe Wyatt."

She looked up at him, lips curving into a smile. "Nice to meet you in person, Joe Wyatt."

He hesitated only a moment before he took her hand, his fingers closing around hers. Her skin was cool, her palm soft, and yet he felt a tingle of heat and he dropped her hand to reach for her roller bag. "Is this all you have?"

"No, I've got two big checked bags coming. They said it shouldn't take long."

"It doesn't, not here. It's not a big airport," he said, looking down at her. Her aviator-style sunglasses reflected his own image, and Joe thought it peculiar that she was still wearing sunglasses inside. He wasn't sure if it was a California thing, or something else, but then, as if she could read his mind, she removed the reflective glasses and slid them into a pocket of her jean jacket before shyly glancing up at him. That was when he saw her brown eyes were watery. Her long black lashes were wet. She'd been crying.

His gut tightened and he felt another kick of disappointment, along with a whisper of concern because she'd ended a serious relationship in the last year. He'd wondered if she was ready for a commitment so soon after that relationship had ended, but she'd assured him she was ready.

Tears worried him, though. Not because he couldn't handle emotions, but Joe spent most of his day out on the property. He wasn't available to do a lot of comfort and conversation. His future wife had to be strong, independent. Self-sufficient. She needed to be low maintenance as well.

Sophie had presented herself as all of that, and more, having been raised on a large family dairy farm, familiar with the long hours her father and brothers worked. But seeing her here in front of him, he had serious reservations.

The tension inside of him hardened into a ball inside his gut, even as a little voice in his head said this wasn't a great start. *Too soft*, he mentally added to the earlier concerns of too pretty, too glossy. She'd never survive life on the ranch, and what he needed was a pragmatic, level-headed woman, who didn't mind isolation or hard work.

He wanted to give her the benefit of the doubt, though. Perhaps something had happened on the flight. Maybe she'd just gotten bad news. "Everything okay?" he asked gruffly.

She nodded, smiling unsteadily. "Yes. Everything okay at your end?"

"Yes, now that you're here. Let's go find those bags of yours."

They didn't talk much as they waited at the baggage carousel for her suitcases and the silence felt awkward. Joe shifted his weight from foot to foot, trying not to read too much into the silence, thinking it was inevitable there'd be some initial awkwardness. She was here in his world; he was responsible for her.

Joe considered the different things he could say and finally asked about her flight. She said it was fine. He struggled to think of something else to say. "Was the plane crowded?"

"Every seat filled," she answered, before adding, "but it's a small plane."

He nodded. More silence stretched, and it felt heavier and even less comfortable than before.

Sophie excused herself to use the ladies' room and when she returned he noticed she'd put some makeup on, covering the traces of her earlier tears. She was so pretty she didn't need makeup, but he took the mascara and whatever else she did to be a sign that the tears were behind her.

Her suitcases arrived a few minutes later and he tucked the smaller roller bag under his arm, pulling the two big cases through the terminal doors to the street. "Wait here while I drive the truck around," he told her. "No sense dragging you and your bags through the parking lot. It's pretty dirty from the melting snow."

"You just had snow?"

"It's pretty much gone now, but it's made everything muddy. I'll be right back." And then he was off, walking quickly, wanting to put distance between them so he could regroup before they were trapped in the car for the next forty-five minutes.

SOPHIE WATCHED JOE Wyatt walk away from her, her

stomach doing mad panicked somersaults, one after the other. What was she doing? What was she thinking?

This was insane. She wasn't impulsive, wasn't prone to mad adventures, and yet here she was, and it was definitely crazy. She didn't know this man. She was in the middle of nowhere, and she was going to get in his truck? Drive to an even more remote nowhere?

He could be an ax-murderer.

He could chain her up in a basement—

Sophie stopped herself, queasy.

She needed to calm down, fast. She'd done her research. She'd made calls, talked to ranchers, business owners and everyone liked the Wyatts; Joe, in particular. Everyone described them as honest, hardworking, trustworthy. The oldest son, Joe, might be a bit gruff and standoffish, but he was a man of integrity, with neighbors uniformly describing him as a good man.

But what did that mean?

What did she really know?

She should go. She should get on the next flight out of Bozeman and head home. She didn't need to marry now. There'd be other opportunities later. Maybe.

And just like that, she pictured Leo, who was supposed to have married her, and the gorgeous, wildly expensive wedding dress which had briefly hung in her closet, and fresh shame and hurt burned through her, just as hot and fresh as it had been when Leo had betrayed her.

For a moment, Sophie couldn't breathe, her chest squeezing tightly with endless pain.

Worse, Leo was now part of her family. Leo would forever be part of her family. If she returned to her family in California.

She didn't have to return home, though, if she ran back into the airport. She could jump on a plane and go anywhere. She could get a job in a different city... have a different life... a new life.

A big black truck pulled up in front of her and shifted into park. The driver door swung open and Joe climbed out and came around to meet her on the curb. His eyes met hers beneath the brim of his cowboy hat. He was taller than she'd expected, bigger, with broad shoulders, long legs, and a disarmingly square jaw.

"You okay?" he asked, eyes narrowing, expression grim.

He struck her as hard. Resolute.

Nothing like Leo, and that was good. Leo was a salesman—literally, VP of sales with his family's company, Brazer Farms—and he was all about charm, being the favorite one.

She forced a smile. "Yes, I'm good. Thank you."

He didn't look like he believed her. "You were crying when you got off the plane."

"I've never been to Montana before."

He lifted a brow. "And that's why you were crying?"

Sophie flushed, and huffed out an embarrassed laugh, thinking he probably hadn't cried a day in his life. "This is suddenly very real, and very scary."

Joe nodded, his stern expression easing. "I'd be worried about you if you weren't a little nervous. It's not every day one agrees to marry a stranger."

"True." She hesitated. "You said if either of us had doubts at the end of the week, we wouldn't go through with the ceremony." She tipped her head back to look him in the eyes, eyes that were a light cool, clear blue. "You mean that?"

"Yes. I've no intention of marrying someone that isn't going to be happy... much less make my mom unhappy. She's to think this is a love match, and neither of us are going to disillusion her."

Sophie glanced down at her luggage. She'd arrived with two carry-on bags and two big suitcases, everything she'd thought she'd need to start this new life as Joe Wyatt's wife. But Paradise Valley, Montana, was a long way from her family's dairy farm in Tulare, California.

But wasn't that what she'd wanted? A fresh start far from her close-knit community where everyone knew everything about each other, including Sophie's humiliation when her groom ran off with her sister Sarah?

"Your mom knows I'm coming, though?" she asked.

"Yes. Granddad, too."

Joe had told her they both lived at the ranch. Mr. Wyatt had raised his four grandsons after his son, their dad, died in a car accident. "And what have you told them?" she asked.

"We met online and have been talking and messaging

and we've hit it off. So I've invited you out to meet everyone."

It was what he'd told her he'd say, but she was double-checking, wanting to be sure the story hadn't changed. "They'll expect us to be a little... uncomfortable... around each other," she said, looking up at him again, and then away, discomfited by the hard square jaw and the firm press of his lips. "Seeing as it's the first time we've met in real life."

"We've got a week," he said, agreeing with her. "We either make it work in the next seven days, or I'll drive you back here next Thursday and put you on a plane."

"Doesn't sound like there's much wiggle room."

"I'm thirty-three and I need a wife and kids and you're either the right woman, or you're not." He opened the passenger door of the truck for her before loading her luggage into the back of the cab. "It's time we find out."

She stiffened at his brusque tone. "You have to be the right one for me as well. I'm not going to be a doormat. I want a husband who will respect me, and treat me like an equal."

His gaze swept her face, lingering on her eyes and then dropping to her mouth. "It's going to be an interesting week, Sophie. Welcome to Montana."

JOE TURNED ON the radio and let the country music station fill the car with sound while he drove. This was not going well.

On the curb, he'd seen a flash of fire from her, but now Sophie had gone quiet, her expression shuttered, gaze fixed on the road ahead of them.

He told himself it was better this way, they needed to be honest, and not start off with any romantic notions, but it felt like he'd swallowed a rock, seeing her go from uncertain but smiling to all shut down as if she was one of the summer cottages in Paradise Valley that had been boarded up for winter.

But as the miles passed, he felt guilty. He wasn't being very chivalrous. This was his future wife, for goodness' sake. No need to alienate her. "My granddad is on the quiet side. He's pretty reserved. If he doesn't talk, don't take it personally. My mom… she's the talker."

Sophie shot him a curious glance. "She gets along well with your girlfriends?"

"I haven't brought anyone home in years. So this is going to be interesting."

"Is your ranch far?"

"In good weather, like today, it's forty minutes to Marietta from here—that's the nearest proper town to the Diamond W Ranch—and then the ranch house is another thirty-five minutes." He looked at her. "Hungry?"

"A little bit," she admitted. "All I've had today are the pretzels the flight attendant passed out."

"No wonder you're a little cranky."

Her jaw dropped. "Me, cranky? I think you're the one

that's sounding hangry."

He flashed a smile. "Maybe. I wouldn't say no to a burger. What do you like to eat?"

"Everything. I'm not picky."

"I was going to stop in Marietta to pick up supplies at the feed store. We can eat in Marietta, too, if you can wait another half hour."

"Not a problem."

They pulled off the highway and stopped first at the feed store which looked over the railroad tracks. Sophie wandered around the store inspecting the merchandise while Joe headed out back with one of the store clerks. It wasn't that different from feed stores in Tulare County and it seemed that the clerk had already pulled everything Joe needed because by the time she made it back to the register, he was almost done loading up his truck.

He jumped down and quickly brushed his hands off on the back of his Levi's. He wore his jeans the way cowboys did—fitted, tight—and they highlighted his quads and his butt. He had a great butt, at least what she could see of it.

He turned and looked straight at her, his gaze locking with hers through the store window. Had he known she was watching him? Her cheeks suddenly burned, and her stomach did a little flip.

Adrenaline rushed through her, and she forced herself to exit the store and meet him at his truck. "I probably should have helped, shouldn't I?" she said.

"I wouldn't have let you." He went around to the passenger side door and opened it for her. "Let's go eat."

He drove down Marietta's main street and parked in front of an old red brick building. Much of the street was lined with turn-of-the-century brick buildings. It had a western feel, like something one might see in a movie, and she tried to take in everything as she followed Joe to the front door of the restaurant.

The interior walls were exposed brick, and along the back wall was a long counter and counter stools. The waitress seated them at an empty table and placed the menus in front of them promising to be back with waters.

Sophie glanced down at the plastic coated menu. *Main Street Diner.* Joe opened his and then closed it almost as quickly. She glanced at the options. Lots of beef and bison. Roast pork and chicken, too. She closed her menu as the waitress returned.

"Do you know what you want?" Joe asked her as the waitress set their waters down.

She nodded. "Bacon cheeseburger with fries."

He smiled crookedly. "The same," he said to the waitress. "Except I'd like my burger rare, and my fries extra crispy."

"Anything to drink?" the waitress asked.

"Coffee," Joe said.

Sophie handed her menu to the waitress. "A Diet Coke for me."

SHE WAITED FOR the waitress to leave to speak. "I know I probably didn't make a great impression, getting off the plane crying. I promise I didn't cry the entire flight. I just teared up as we were landing. I don't know why I got emotional, either. I'm sure you're just as nervous as I am—maybe more—because you're taking me home. This can't be easy for you, bringing me into your world, and now you have to introduce me to both your mom and your grandfather."

"I'm not that nervous."

"No?"

"I know what I'm doing. I just wonder… if you do."

She glanced down at her hands where she'd knotted her fingers together. "I want this, too. I'm thirty in a few months and my biological clock is ticking and I'm ready to start a family." She hesitated. "I want to start a family with you."

He smiled and, when he did, it was megawatt, with white teeth and a glimpse of a dimple that fascinated her. "Sounds like a plan."

When their food arrived, they mostly concentrated on eating, and Sophie tried to relax and not think about what would come next. It was one thing to have a burger with a stranger in a public place. It was another to go home with him, and to become utterly dependent on him. He said he lived at a fairly high elevation, that their ranch had beautiful views of the Yellowstone River, but they weren't close to anything.

"How far to your nearest neighbor?" she asked him as they left the diner and headed to his truck.

"Fifteen minutes, maybe."

"So you didn't grow up playing with your neighbors."

"I had my brothers. We did everything together."

Sophie was glued to her window as they left Marietta, eager to see the famed Paradise Valley which she'd read a lot about after investigating the Wyatt family. Paradise Valley had originally drawn miners, and then ranchers, and now celebrities and affluent Americans bought up large parcels of land for their own piece of the West.

"Do you have any celebrities near you?" she asked, as Joe left Highway 89 and began driving toward the mountains.

"No. They prefer the valley floor and the foothills. We're rather inhospitable where we are."

It didn't take long for Sophie to realize Joe hadn't been exaggerating when he said the Wyatt ranch was high in the Gallatins. Sophie felt as if they'd been climbing and climbing, the narrow, gravel road winding up and around the mountain, for miles. In places, the narrow road was swallowed by a thicket of poplar trees, but at every turn there was a jaw-dropping view of the valley. If the road felt steep and treacherous in spring, she couldn't imagine navigating this in winter with all the snow and ice and wind.

She chewed on her bottom lip, fighting yet another flurry of nerves as it crossed her mind that she might have overplayed her agricultural background. Yes, she was the daughter of a dairy farmer, but she'd been raised to work in the front office, not in the dairy barns. Her brothers did that. She and her sister helped their mom with the business side, and there was plenty of it, but it was comfortable work, in a comfortable office. Her gaze slid across the rocky mountain with scattered pine trees and patches of lingering snow and tried to imagine what she'd do here, and how she'd help Joe. What was the life of a Montana cowboy wife?

"Are we on your land yet?" she asked.

"Ever since the cattle guard a mile back. The Diamond W Ranch property line extends to the top of the mountain, giving us seven thousand acres total."

"How do your cattle survive winters up here?"

"We move them to our lowest pastures in October, and feed them daily. Granddad and I will be taking them back up in just a couple weeks." He shot her a glance. "We still take hay and feed up a couple times a week."

"You must envy the ranchers on the lower slopes."

"I don't really think of it that way. This property has been in the family four generations. My grandfather was raised here, my dad was raised here, and I've lived here since I was almost eight. This is home, simple as that."

It wasn't a rebuke and yet she felt the distance grow between them.

Or, maybe it was her own fear making her shut down and retreat.

She didn't want to be afraid, though, and she didn't

want him to second-guess his decision—not yet. She had to pull herself together, had to show him who she really was. Smart, self-sufficient, successful. She'd spent the past five years managing the import/export business for Brazer Farms, one of Central California's largest dried fruit growers, and she'd grown their business, and figured out ways to cut waste, making the company even more profitable. She loved positive returns on investment. She loved to see how she could make a difference. That was what had appealed to her about Joe's ad. He'd wanted a wife, and a partner, someone to help him ensure the success of his ranch for the next generation. Having come from a family that was a multigenerational business, she understood the values, and the history, of a family business, and she was looking forward to becoming part of his.

"Tell me about your mom again. You said she's become frail, and isn't as mobile as she used to be. What happened to her?" she asked. "If you don't mind telling me?"

"She has rheumatoid arthritis," he said. "She was diagnosed in her early thirties and it's not going to get better. She's increasingly dependent on those around her." Joe glanced at her before focusing again on the rough gravel road. "You're not coming to be her nurse. If and when she needs an aide, I'll hire one. She hasn't had an easy life, and her happiness means a great deal to me."

"I understand."

"It will be an adjustment for her, having another woman

in her house, in her kitchen."

"Does she still cook then?"

"She wishes she could, but no. She's not very mobile. You'll see she uses a cane, but even then her balance isn't good. Granddad and I do most of the cooking—well, mostly me now. It's not great, but we're not starving."

Her gaze swept over him. He most definitely wasn't starving. The man was built, with muscles and more muscles. "I'll be happy to take over cooking," she said, "if that makes things easier for you and your family, although I can't promise that my food will taste much better than yours."

A solid two-story log cabin home came into view with a large barn off to one side. The house looked solid and sprawling, with wings off the original structure, and covered porches wrapping the entire lower level. A series of six dormer windows lined the second floor, the windows tall to allow sunlight deep into the room. The metal green roof was steep, and looked new against the weathered logs of the house. A tree in the front had a few bright green leaves but most of the shrubs and roses planted near the front door were still dormant.

In the distance, Sophie could hear barking.

"Home, sweet home," Joe said, braking, slowing. "You always have to be careful as you get near the house. The dogs like to chase cars."

"Dogs?"

The sound of barking grew louder. He pointed to what

looked like a pack of dogs racing toward them. Two big black-and-gold German shepherds and a blonde Lab. Sophie stiffened and held her breath, trying not to be alarmed. She wasn't a fan of big, working dogs.

"What's wrong?" he asked, glancing at her. "You don't like dogs?"

"I don't dislike cute fluffy dogs, but I was bit by a German shepherd when I was little." She held up her hand, showing a faint line. "I had to get stitches. It was pretty scary."

"Our dogs won't hurt you. They just get excited to see cars." He shifted into park in front of the imposing house, and turned off the engine. "But at the same time, you can't act scared. You have to be the dominant one. Dogs sense fear—"

"I'll be fine," she interrupted, not wanting him to think she was a total sissy. "Don't worry."

He pointed to each of the barking, circling dogs. "That's Penny, Duke, and Runt."

"Penny is the Lab?" she asked.

"Yes."

"And Runt is the smaller shepherd?"

He laughed, amused, the sound a low rumble in his chest. "No, Runt's the big one. The dogs are from the same litter. Runt wasn't supposed to survive but he turned out to be one fine dog." He swung his door open. "Sit tight and I'll come around, introduce you to the dogs, and then take you into the house. Once you're in the house, they'll calm down. Runt is very protective to the property and boundaries. Once you're in the house with me, he'll realize you're supposed to be there."

"But until then he'll want to take my head off?" she said with a weak laugh.

"Something like that. But if it's any comfort, I don't think he's actually ever bit anyone. He just gets real close."

"Doesn't really make me feel better."

"Just remember, be the alpha."

Joe climbed out behind the steering wheel, put cowboy boots on the ground, and slammed his door closed. Sophie watched him scratch the dogs' heads, and behind the ears, before giving each of them big pats. The dogs wagged their tails, howled with pleasure. *It's okay. They don't actually bite. You're going to be fine. Act confident.*

"Be the alpha."

Runt lunged forward but Joe issued a sharp command and the big dog sat down immediately.

"Ignore Runt," Joe instructed. "Focus on Penny. Call her and she'll come to you, and she's very gentle. Lavish her with attention, and pretend Runt doesn't exist. The fact that you're spoiling Penny will make Runt wildly jealous. The longer you ignore him the more he'll want to be your friend. Trust me, by the end of the week, he'll be eating out of your hand."

So, Sophie did exactly what Joe told her. She called Penny over, and scratched her head, and behind her ear, and told her how pretty she was in her best crooning voice, and when Sophie looked up, she saw Runt watching intently, so intently, she thought Joe was right. Runt looked a little jealous.

The interior of the log cabin was much like the rustic exterior, split logs, lots of wood, and a stacked stone chimney. Joe's tour of the house was brief—this is the downstairs, this is the upstairs, this will be your room—before she was taken to the family room to meet his mother.

"Mom, this is Sophie. Sophie, my mom, Summer Wyatt. She was born in California but has lived in Montana for twenty-some years now."

Summer Wyatt probably once fit her name. Even now, Mrs. Wyatt was pretty, a fine-boned faded blonde, reminiscent of sun-baked flowers in the hot part of August. She had hazel eyes and a generous mouth, and wore her long silver-streaked blonde hair in a loose side braid.

"Nice to meet you, Sophie. Where about in California are you from?" She shot Joe an unsmiling side glance. "Joe hasn't told us much about you."

"A small town called Tulare. It's in Central California, halfway between Fresno and Bakersfield."

"Home of Bob Mathias, the Olympic champion," Summer said.

"That's right."

"So what brings you to Montana?" Mrs. Wyatt said, not

missing a beat. "I'm sure you didn't come out all this way just to see Joe."

Sophie shot Joe a quick look. "But I did." She struggled to hold her smile. "We've been messaging back and forth and I thought it was time to meet."

"Only messaging?"

"No, we had some calls and we FaceTimed."

"And now you're here," Mrs. Wyatt said, and from her tone, it was clear she wasn't happy.

Sophie's heart fell but she wasn't about to let her disappointment show. "Two flights later, plus an hour drive from Bozeman." She kept smiling as she looked at Joe. "But look at him—he's worth it."

CHAPTER TWO

I T WASN'T GOING well.

Dinner was stiff and conversation stilted. Joe found it hard to chew the roast; the moist meat might as well have been sawdust in his mouth. He was aware this wasn't the norm at the dinner table. He'd known his grandfather would be reserved, but he hadn't expected his mom to be cold and unwelcoming. He actually felt sorry for Sophie, wishing he'd better prepared her, but Sophie was earning his respect by keeping her cool despite the chilly welcome. He didn't know how she managed to be smiling right now, but he appreciated her cheerfulness more than she knew.

"That was delicious," she said, as Joe rose to clear the dinner plates. "Thank you so much, Mrs. Wyatt."

"Glad you enjoyed it," his mom answered with a tight smile. "But thanks should go to Joe. He put it in the oven before he went to collect you."

Joe counted to three, and then five, as he stacked the plates and dirty cutlery. His mom was about as warm as an iceberg. "Coffee, anyone?" he asked. "We've got some lemon cake, too. I picked it up from the bakery this afternoon."

"Nothing for me," Granddad said. "I've got a show I want to watch."

"None for me," his mom chimed in, even though every night she drank a cup of black coffee after the meal. It was her evening ritual.

"You're sure, Mom?" he asked, standing in the doorway. "You love Rachel's lemon cake."

"I'm sure." She gave him another strained smile, and he cursed inwardly, baffled and frustrated by the wall she'd put up tonight. "But thank you, Joe. I might have a slice of that lemon cake for breakfast."

Joe turned to Sophie. "Sophie, what about you? Coffee? Tea? We have some herbal tea in there somewhere if you prefer that."

"I'm good, thank you. Let me help you clear," she said, rising and reaching for the platter.

His mom's hand flew out, stopping Sophie. "Don't do that, Sophie, sit. Please."

Sophie hesitated, forehead creasing. "I'd like to help. I'm not used to being waited on."

"That might be true, but guests don't work, not in my house," his mother answered, smiling tightly.

Joe couldn't remember when he was last so uncomfortable. He loved and respected his mom, but he was so disappointed in her right now, and ashamed that his family wasn't being more welcoming to Sophie.

Sophie glanced from his mom to him. "But it's not

work," she replied. "I'm grateful—"

"Sophie," Joe interrupted, quietly. "It's okay, I've got this. I'll be right back."

SOPHIE SAT BACK down at the table, exhaling silently. She wouldn't call dinner miserable, but it hadn't been fun. Joe had carried most of the conversation, talking about general subjects like the weather, his brothers who were competing around now on the professional rodeo circuit, and if any of them might make an appearance for Easter which was less than two weeks away. She'd asked when his brothers had last been home, and his mom had said they always came home every year for Christmas, which must have meant that the three younger Wyatt brothers hadn't been home since December. It was hard to say.

Joe's grandfather, Melvin—whom Joe rather resembled if aged forty plus years—pushed up from the table, excusing himself, leaving Sophie and Mrs. Wyatt alone together.

Joe's mom didn't try to make conversation, though, and they both sat at the table in silence. Sophie hated it. She suddenly wondered how any of this was going to work. What had she gotten into, coming to Montana, agreeing to marry Joe and live on his family's ranch?

Joe returned then, emerging through the swinging door from the kitchen. He came to stand behind her chair, his knuckles lightly brushing her shoulder, letting her know he was there.

But she knew he was there. Joe had an intensely masculine energy that made her aware of him the moment he entered or left a room. She could feel him behind her now, his energy so potent it felt as if he was still touching her.

"Mom, is there anything I can do for you before I steal Sophie away?" he asked.

Mrs. Wyatt's gaze swept over her and then lifted to look at her son. "Where are you going?"

"Thought I'd grab Sophie's luggage from the truck and get her settled in. She's had a long day. I'm sure she'd be happy to just unpack and relax."

Mrs. Wyatt's hand clenched where it rested on the dining table. "Could we have a minute, Joe?" She glanced to Sophie. "Would you mind, dear?"

"Not at all," Sophie said, sliding out of her chair. "I can go outside—"

"Not outside," Joe interrupted. "It's cold. And Runt might make you nervous. The family room would be better. Granddad's in there watching TV."

"I don't want to interfere with his show," Sophie answered. "What if I wait in the kitchen?"

Joe nodded and she slipped out, but even with the swinging door closed, Sophie could hear Mrs. Wyatt's voice. There didn't seem to be a way to escape the conversation.

"I don't know what you're thinking, Joe. Springing this on us. Why wouldn't you tell us?"

"I did tell you," he answered. "You knew I was going to Bozeman to pick her up from the airport."

"But I didn't know she would be staying *here*."

"Come on, Mom, that's not true. You knew I'd changed the sheets on Sam's bed, and opened the windows to air the room out."

Silence fell, the silence too long to be anything good.

"So how long *is* she staying?" his mother asked.

Exasperation sharpened Joe's tone. "I don't know. Does it matter?"

Sophie couldn't hear his mother's answer, or maybe Mrs. Wyatt didn't answer. Either way, a heaviness filled her, making her stomach hurt. This wasn't what she'd expected. She didn't know what she expected, but it certainly wasn't… *this*.

It wasn't that long before Joe found her in the kitchen. His expression was grim, his hard jaw set. Sophie could see how unhappy he was; he wasn't unhappy with her, but with his family, and that didn't bode well… not for them, not for the future.

"It's okay," she said softly. "It really is."

"You heard?" he asked.

"Enough to know that me being here is a problem."

"I'm sorry."

"It's fine."

"No, it's not." He turned away, paced the floor. "I live here, work here, rarely leave here," he said, almost under his breath. "I'm chained to this place, body and soul, and it shouldn't be an issue for me to invite someone here."

"But it is," she answered, "and we just need to adjust our plans. We don't want to add to the tension. If your mom is this resistant to me visiting, how will she ever reconcile herself to the news that we're getting married?"

He abruptly stopped pacing. "Let's go outside and talk. I'll get your coat."

The log cabin house had a long covered veranda that ran the length of the house. A pair of rocking chairs were pushed up against one end of the wall while a bench was against another. Joe chose to sit on the railing instead, facing her, arms again bundled over his chest.

He didn't say anything for a long moment. He stared at a point just over his head, jaw set, eyes narrowed, expression grim. "Sorry. I hate that this is so damn awkward right now. I hate that they're making you uncomfortable."

"You're uncomfortable too," she said. "And this isn't going to work if everyone's upset, because here's what I know. You're loyal to your family, just as you should be. You and I are strangers. We don't have history. We don't have a relationship—"

"But we will," he interrupted.

"With time."

Joe didn't reply to that, and Sophie watched him, concerned. She'd been through so much these last few months that this tension, this awkwardness, in the big picture was nothing. This wasn't personal either. She had a feeling his mom would react this way to any woman coming into the house. His mom was afraid of being replaced, and having an outsider—a young woman—here was a threat to her and her comfortable routines. Sophie represented change, and from the sound of it, there hadn't been a lot of change here at the Wyatts' ranch in a very long time.

"What if I go stay at a hotel in town, and give your family time to adjust?" she suggested. "There's no reason I need to stay here. I suppose it was unrealistic to think I could just appear and settle in right away."

Joe didn't answer; he just stared out over the dark valley, a small muscle pulling in his chiseled jaw.

She watched him a moment before continuing. "It's not as if we were going to spend all of our time together these next few days. You're going to be on the property working during the day. I was going to be here at the house with your mom. But I can see why she's nervous having me here. You are quite isolated up here and she's probably worrying about having to entertain me. Why would she want to be alone with a stranger all day? If I were in her shoes, I might feel the same."

"You're being very magnanimous," he said roughly, shooting her an indecipherable look.

"This is her home. She shouldn't feel uncomfortable in her own home."

"She could have been more diplomatic. Granddad, too."

Sophie shrugged. "Honestly, I far prefer people saying how they feel, than hiding it, or covering it up." She couldn't help remembering all the ways Leo kept the truth from her, and all the ways his silence betrayed her. "It's always better to know where you stand, than have people try to protect you by keeping the truth from you."

"I agree with you on that."

"You know, this is probably a blessing in disguise. I'm actually a little relieved. It gives us a chance to get to know each other without being on top of each other or your family." The dogs suddenly came barreling toward them out of the dark, and Sophie stiffened as they raced up the stairs. Joe uttered a sharp command and the dogs promptly sat.

"They're good dogs," Joe said.

She nodded weakly. "Yes."

"They like you," he insisted.

She eyed Runt who had to be the biggest German shepherd she'd ever seen in her life. "I'll take your word for it."

Joe smiled crookedly and rose from the railing. "All right. Let's do this. Back to Marietta we go."

JOE MADE CALLS on their way to town, using his truck's Bluetooth on the speaker so Sophie could hear the options. He called the biggest and nicest hotel in town, the Graff, first, and the Graff had rooms but they were pricey and Sophie shook her head. He then phoned a couple of the bed-

and-breakfasts. The first two B&B's were booked up since it was apparently spring break somewhere, but Bramble House just had a room open. It was a small room with a shared bath, but Sophie mouthed that she didn't mind so Joe asked that they save the room for her, as they were on their way to town now.

"That's a cute name," Sophie said after he hung up. "Bramble House."

"It's the first big mansion ever built in Marietta. Big red brick with lots of windows and white trim. Built sometime in the 1880s, I believe. The Brambles were also the founders of the big bank in town. Up until last fall, the bank was still a bank. It's just recently been closed and sold."

"You know a lot of history."

"That's probably all the history I know."

"I'd love to learn more about Montana."

"There's a whole display at the library, which is really close to Bramble House. In fact, everything is close to Bramble House. You'll be able to walk to town from where you're staying."

Fifteen minutes later, he parked his truck in front of the old red brick mansion and lifted Sophie's luggage out of the back. "Thoughts?" he said.

"I like it," she said, smiling.

Indeed, she seemed charmed by Bramble House during the brief check-in. When he carried her suitcases up to her room, he thought it was small, but she proclaimed it perfect, and gave the antique bed positioned underneath the steep eaves a little bounce before sitting next in the emerald-green overstuffed armchair and curling her legs under her. "I love it."

He arched a brow. "You don't have to sell it that hard."

"I'm serious. It's lovely. I've never stayed anyplace like this."

"No?"

"I feel like I'm on vacation," she said.

Considering the long day she'd had, she looked happy and almost unbearably pretty. "I appreciate your flexibility," he said, "more than you know."

"We knew there would be hiccups. This is just one of them."

He opened his mouth to protest and then thought better of it. "Anything you need before I go?"

"No. I'm fine. Exhausted, but fine. I'm going to sleep like a baby tonight."

"I hope so."

"Don't worry about me. I know you have things waiting at home, needing your attention, so let me walk you down."

"You stay put. I can see myself out. Good night, Sophie."

"Good night, Joe." She hesitated, suddenly looking less sure of herself. "Will you call me tomorrow?"

"I'll see you tomorrow," he answered firmly. "And thank you," he added, walking out.

Joe found himself thinking about Sophie the entire drive

home. She'd seemed fragile and emotional at the airport, and rather quiet and self-contained during the drive to his ranch, but when confronted by a chilly welcome, she'd handled herself well. It was obvious to him her first concern was his family, and making everyone else comfortable, and he respected her for that. It was something he would do— something he did do—and it was reassuring to see that they shared some of the same values. But if she valued family so much, and if family was so important to her, why had she chosen to leave hers and move halfway across the country to start over?

SOPHIE WAS IN bed, lights out, close to finally falling asleep when her phone rang. She never got calls late at night and she reached for her phone on the nightstand. It was Sarah, her sister. Sophie felt a pang, hurt colored with a terrible sadness. She and Sarah had once been close, but her betrayal with Leo cut deep. Sophie wasn't sure if she and Sarah would ever be close again, much less friends again. Sarah was her sister so she couldn't hate her, but she certainly didn't like her.

She put the phone back on the nightstand, without answering. Sarah could either leave a message or not. If it was serious there would be a voicemail. If it was Sarah just trying to apologize, she could save her breath. Sophie didn't want an apology. She wanted life the way it used to be. She wanted life where she trusted people, especially her sister. Never mind her fiancé.

Sophie and Leo had been together for years. It wasn't like they had some whirlwind romance and fell in love on an impulse. No, they'd been dating for almost three years, and engaged for a year. How and when did Leo fall out of love with Sophie and in love with Sarah instead?

Sophie mashed the pillow beneath her cheek, her insides churning, heart on fire again.

She was so tired of feeling this way. She was so tired of feeling hurt and angry and guilty and sad and disappointed. That was why she'd answered the ad and come to Montana. It was why she was so determined to marry Joe and start a new life.

New hopes, new possibilities.

New home.

New family.

Joe might never love her, but if he was kind to her, and respectful... if he didn't cheat on her and break her heart... if he was honest, hardworking, and loving with their children that would be a good life. That would be a life she'd be proud of. Romantic love was no longer important.

She wanted honesty, integrity. *Truth*.

And love? Well, that was terribly overrated, because love shouldn't wound and hurt. Love shouldn't break her heart. Love shouldn't have made her feel absolutely... worthless.

❦

THE MORNING ARRIVED bright and clear with a strong brisk breeze. After breakfast, and armed with a small walking map provided by Eliza Bramble, Sophie headed for the big park with the library and courthouse to look for the walking path that followed the river. She walked a good mile and a half, enjoying the view of the mountains in the morning sun gleaming on snowcapped Copper Mountain. She used her little map to identify buildings and landmarks. Crawford Park. The rodeo and fairgrounds. Marietta's hospital.

She came back a different way, walking through a poorer side of town, before crossing the railroad tracks and passing the four-story red brick Graff Hotel, which Joe had called last night to check on availability and rates. She could see why it'd been so expensive. Peeking through the front doors, the lobby was all rich paneled woods and gleaming marble. Definitely a posh place for Marietta.

Descending the hotel steps, she headed to the handsome old train depot which was closed at the moment but looked like it had been reimagined as a restaurant and bar before crossing Front Street to check out the movie theater, the menu taped in the window of the Chinese restaurant, and then the colorful display of formal gowns in *Married in Marietta*, the local bridal store. The vivid hues of the gowns in the store window told her it must be almost prom season. There was a sign near the front door that said *Help Wanted*, and Sophie shuddered, thinking that would be the worst job in the world.

She no longer had her wedding dress—she'd asked one of the women she worked with to donate it somewhere, perhaps to a charity that could get some money for it—but she could still picture the gorgeous white silk, the fitted bodice, and exquisite beading on the full skirt. It had been an impossibly expensive gown, just as everything in her wedding had been elegant and lavish. Looking back, it was a ridiculous waste of money, but when planning the wedding, it had seemed so romantic and special the cost hadn't troubled her.

Maybe that was another reason marrying Joe at the courthouse, or flying to Las Vegas for a chapel ceremony there, appealed.

No fuss. No flowers. No white gowns with long lace veils.

Just the vows, the commitment, the marriage.

Sophie's phone rang. She hunched her shoulders and ignored it, suspecting it was Sarah again. She walked down a block and headed for Main Street, and only checked the phone after it stopped ringing. She was wrong, though. It hadn't been Sarah, it was Joe.

She called him back.

"Good morning," he said, when he answered.

"Walking back to Bramble House. I've been out exploring."

"Where did you go?"

"Everywhere. I started with the library, and then the courthouse in Crawford Park and went along the river, and then over the bridge. I saw pretty much everything."

"Marietta must seem small to you."

"Not really. It's actually bigger than I thought. When we came yesterday I thought Marietta was just Main Street, but there's so much more to the town. What are you doing?"

"I've taken care of all the morning chores and thinking that I'd come into town and meet you for lunch. Are you free?"

"Is that a trick question? I have nothing to do. I'm only here in Montana for you."

For a moment, there was just silence and then Joe spoke, his voice deeper than before. "I like the sound of that. I'll pick you up at noon."

SOPHIE SHOWERED AND washed her hair, taking pains to blow it dry so that it was straight. If she hadn't straightened it, it'd be long unruly curls, and left to their own devices the curls would get bigger and wilder and impossible to manage. Far better to straighten her hair into submission, just the way she wanted to get control of her life. It was time to be practical. Efficient. Time to show fate she was the boss.

But checking her phone, she spotted a text from her mom. "*I just heard you left your job at Brazer Farms, and that you've sold your condo, too. Is it true?*" Sophie felt a sharp twinge in her chest. She hadn't wanted to deceive her mom, but at the same time, how could she continue working for

Leo's family? There was no future for her with Brazer Farms, no future with the Brazer family, and no need for a condo two miles from the Brazer Farms headquarters.

She texted her mom back. "*I didn't want to worry you. But everything is good, I promise.*"

Her mom wasn't satisfied. "*Where are you?*"

Sophie hesitated then texted, "*Montana.*"

Her mom answered immediately. "*WHAT!?! Why?*"

"*I had a*"—Sophie paused, thinking carefully about her word choice, before continuing—"*opportunity in Montana and I'm here exploring options.*"

Her phone buzzed a new text, this one from Joe. "*Here.*"

"*On my way down,*" she answered him, before texting her mom, "*I need to go, but I'll call you soon. Love you. Xo*"

CLIMBING INTO JOE'S truck, Sophie could immediately tell he wasn't in a good mood despite the smile he flashed at her.

"Hey," she said, closing the door and reaching for her seat belt. "Everything okay?"

He nodded and gave her another tight smile. "Great."

Her field of work was dominated by men and she had three brothers, giving her plenty of experience with the adult male and it was clear that Joe was anything but great, but she didn't know him well enough to know if she should push for more, or let it go. In the end, she decided—for now—to let it go. He'd talk to her if he wanted.

"How did you sleep?" he asked, shifting into drive.

"Good." She watched him a moment, intrigued by his profile with the flat brows, straight nose, firm mouth, hard defined chin. Photos hadn't done him justice. He was handsome... rugged. Cowboy handsome. The kind of man that thrilled her, but also intimidated her because he wasn't extroverted or with a laidback charm like Leo. Joe struck her as a man who held everything in, keeping his cards close to his chest. "The bed was perfect, and the breakfast was amazing. Muffins and coffee cake, eggs, fruit, potatoes. I ate enough for two."

The corner of Joe's mouth lifted. "You're making me hungry, but I suppose after all of that, you're not ready for lunch."

"Oh, I am," she answered cheerfully. "That was hours ago."

"Good. We're heading to Livingston to pick up a horse trailer for my brother and I thought we'd grab lunch there before heading home."

"I'm all in."

He glanced at her, his gaze sweeping her face before he smiled properly, a smile that warmed his light blue eyes. "Yes, you are, and I have to say, I like that about you."

The drive to Livingston took about twenty minutes and they stopped downtown at Pinky's Café for sandwiches before continuing on to a ranch further north off of Highway 89. When Joe had said he needed to pick up a horse trailer, Sophie had pictured the typical small two horse trailer, but it was a huge luxurious trailer with spacious living quarters and stalls for three horses.

"Which of your brothers is buying the horse trailer?"

"Sam."

"And which one is he?"

"He's the next oldest. It goes me, Sam, Billy, Tommy."

"He must be doing pretty well."

"He is, but they all are. All three of them went to the NFRs in Las Vegas last year." He paused. "And the year before." He saw her blank expression. "That's good; it's the championship, rather like the Super Bowl for professional rodeo cowboys."

"That *is* good."

He looked amused. "You don't know much about the rodeo?"

She shook her head. "No. There were guys at my high school who roped, and wore their Wranglers and boots and western shirts religiously, but we were in different classes and activities so I didn't really pay them much attention."

"You weren't into FFA or any of the other clubs?"

"I attended a couple meetings my freshman year but it wasn't for me. My brothers belonged, though. My oldest brother, John, was really active. I think he was president or something like that his senior year. He's the one that runs our dairy business now and is on the board for the California Dairy Association."

Sophie stayed out of the way while Joe hitched the huge

trailer. He did it almost effortlessly, though, lining up the trailer and coupler on the first try. Next he attached the safety chains and cables and then the wiring harness and finally the safety cables. "Sam's planning on converting this to a gooseneck trailer," Joe said, as he finished. "It's why he got such a good deal on it."

"That's nice of you to get it for him."

"Happy to help. I'm looking forward to seeing him."

"I take it you're probably closest to him?"

"We used to be close, but it's changed since I stopped competing and returned home. The other three travel together a lot and are pretty tight."

"You were a rodeo cowboy, too?"

He looked almost embarrassed. "For a while there."

"How long?"

"Five years."

"Wow. So impressive. Were you good?"

"I've won my share of championship buckles." There was pride in his voice, but also something else.

She glanced at him, curious. "Why did you give it up? Did you get hurt?"

"I was needed at home." He adjusted his cowboy hat. "Speaking of home, we better get on the road. It's going to be slower traveling pulling this rig."

"And I'm sure you have work waiting for you on the ranch."

"Always," he agreed, a hint of weariness in his deep voice.

CHAPTER THREE

O N THE DRIVE back to Marietta, Sophie wrestled with herself, wanting to ask Joe about the future and their plans. Was everything still on? Were they still going to marry in a week's time, or were they working off a different time frame now?

For some reason, she felt uneasy and she wasn't sure why. Everything was good between them today, better than their strained lunch yesterday and tense dinner last night. She shouldn't be nervous. They'd had a nice lunch today, conversation was natural, there was nothing that should make her worried—she stopped herself.

That wasn't true.

She was worried because she wasn't on the ranch, and she had been relegated to town, and although at the moment everything with her and Joe was fine, she worried other things might soon change.

Butterflies filled her middle, and Sophie drew a slow breath, trying to settle her nerves. She wished she knew for certain everything would work out. It'd be so much easier to let go, and not feel like she had to seize control. But control was illusory, wasn't it?

It had never crossed her mind that she couldn't trust Leo. She'd believed in him—in them—implicitly. They'd worked together for years. They'd practically been living together the last eighteen months of their relationship. Yes, he still had his own place, but he spent every night, every weekend at hers.

Sophie shifted restlessly on the truck seat, glancing out her passenger window at the scenery even as she blinked back stupid tears.

She was done with love. Done with romance. She didn't trust pretty words and gifts of candy and flowers. Gifts were easy to give. She wanted something more substantial, something lasting. She wanted security, permanence. Forever.

When she agreed to come to Montana to marry Joe, she'd already made a commitment to him. In her mind, she was committed, and she'd arrived expecting things to be settled. She'd expected more stability.

And now Joe was driving her back to Bramble House and she didn't know when she'd see him again. Would it be tonight for dinner? Would he try to break away from the ranch to see her tomorrow? How often would they see each other? How long would it take for him to realize he didn't want her after all?

Emotion thickened the lump in her throat and made her chest burn. She'd given up her job and sold her condo to be here. Had she made a mistake? She didn't know… but then, she didn't know anything anymore.

JOE WATCHED SOPHIE from the corner of his eye. She looked troubled and it worried him.

He should just ask her what was wrong, but he wasn't sure he was ready for her answer, or the possibility of tears. He wasn't good with drama, and his mom had been incredibly difficult this morning. They'd had an argument before he left to pick up Sophie for lunch, and while he loved his mom, he wasn't a boy, and his mom was in no position to give ultimatums. He understood better than anyone his responsibilities. For heaven's sake, the whole reason he was looking for a wife was for his mother and his grandfather's peace of mind. They'd wanted him to marry years ago, needing to know that there would be grandchildren and future generations on the Wyatt ranch. He was marrying so they'd stop pestering him to date and settle down.

At Bramble House, Joe swung out of the truck to come around and open the door for Sophie. She hopped out and glanced down the street. "You'll be all right getting that big trailer out of here?" she asked him. "It's a pretty narrow street."

"No problem at all. I've got it."

"Okay." She forced a smile, but it didn't reach her eyes. "Thanks for lunch."

"My pleasure. Talk soon."

"Sounds good." And then she was walking up to the bed-and-breakfast as if there was a dragon breathing fire against her back.

Joe kicked himself mentally the whole way home.

He'd handled that badly. He handled *her* badly. If she were a skittish horse he'd be patient. He could afford to be even more patient with her. *Reassuring.*

She'd given up everything to come here, and he should know what that was like. He'd given up everything for this ranch—his career, his love—and he still had regrets. But he also understood duty.

Duty was what had prompted him to place the ad on the website.

Duty was what would see him married next week.

Joe didn't always like himself, but his word was his word, and when he made a promise, he kept it.

JOE CALLED SOPHIE later that afternoon. "I'm not going to be able to make it into town for dinner," he said, his deep voice hard and flat over the line. "And I won't be able to do lunch tomorrow, as Granddad and I will be riding up into the backcountry looking for a couple cows that have gone missing. But we'll be back before dark, and then I'll hop into the shower and change and head into town and we'll get dinner. Sound okay to you?"

It was a long speech for him, Sophie thought, a lot of words strung together and there wasn't really room for her to argue or protest. She wasn't wanted or needed at the ranch, and he wasn't going to be available for a day.

She told herself it didn't hurt.

She told herself it was fine.

But it didn't feel fine.

She felt terrible as a matter of fact. She practically hummed with regret, but there was no way she'd let him know that. "No worries. Be safe tomorrow."

"I will, and we'll have a nice dinner tomorrow."

For a split second, she almost begged him to drive down tonight. For a split second, she almost told him how scared she was, but Sophie's pride kept her from revealing how vulnerable she felt and so she faked a cheerful, "Sounds great, Joe."

"I'm looking forward to it."

Another wave of pain washed over her. What was she doing here? How could she have possibly thought Montana would be the answer? How could she have imagined it'd be so easy to start over?

But Sophie had her pride, so much pride, and so she swallowed hard and blinked back foolish tears. "Me, too."

SO FAR, NOTHING was going the way he'd planned, and Joe felt increasingly frustrated, but he couldn't let his mother know. His mom hated being dependent on others, and she hated that she couldn't cook like she used to or deep clean anymore. She missed driving and grocery shopping and she worried about being a burden, and so Joe juggled his responsibilities tonight, just as he did every night.

As he used the pancake turner to break up the browning ground beef as it sizzled with the diced onions in the cast-iron skillet, he kept an eye on the clock, aware he was getting a later start to town than he'd planned, but so far, he wasn't really late. He could make up some time on the drive, but he wasn't going to be late, because he wasn't going to make Sophie wait. It was bad enough he couldn't see her last night. She'd only just arrived in Montana and yet she was spending all of her time alone.

"You don't have to make dinner before you go," his mom said, slowly entering the kitchen, her cane lightly scarping the wooden floor.

"It's what I do every night, Mom. Just because I'm not eating here, doesn't mean I'm going to leave you and Granddad hungry."

"We could fend for ourselves," she answered, making her way to the breakfast table and carefully sitting down.

"You could, but since I'm here, I might as well get it ready so all you have to do is dish it up when you're hungry." He glanced over his shoulder, taking in his mom's posture. "You're hurting tonight, aren't you?"

"No more than usual."

"I think we should get you back in to see Dr. Johnson."

"He'll just give me more medicine and the medicine will make me sleepy or dizzy or depressed—"

"Is the pain better, Mom?"

"At least I know I'm alive."

"There are other ways to know you're alive," he said, taking a potholder from the counter to wrap the skillet handle before carrying the skillet to the sink. "Pain shouldn't be the measure of one's existence."

She didn't answer him, but he could feel her gaze on him as he drained the fat from the meat. Her gaze felt sharp, pointed, and she dying to say something. Joe wished she'd just come out and say it. It was hard enough communicating with her without the extra silences.

Returning the skillet to the stove, he turned the heat down and dumped in the sour cream and seasonings and gave it a good stir. "The noodles are cooked. This just needs to simmer a few minutes and then you should be good to go." He covered the stroganoff with an oversized lid and turned around. "Anything you need me to do before I head out?"

His mom just looked at him, expression guarded, fine lines etched at her eyes, and yet he could feel her tension, as well as her resistance. She didn't want him to go. She hadn't been happy yesterday evening, either, but tonight she seemed even more upset.

"Just say it, Mom. You know you want to."

"I don't want to fight with you tonight. I was so upset after you left last night."

"Fine. Don't say anything. I need to get on the road. We have a six thirty reservation at Rocco's." He felt his jeans back pocket, wallet, and then his front pocket, keys. Good to go. "See you in the morning," he said, crossing to her, and kissing her forehead. "Don't try to stay up. I might be late." He headed to the back door where the coats were hung up on pegs drilled into the split-log wall.

He was just sliding his coat on when his mother said, "Why her?"

Joe tensed, air bottled in his lungs. This was exactly how it started last night. Right as he tried to walk out. Right as he tried to carve some time for himself. Last night he'd been frustrated. Tonight he was angry.

"Why not her?" he replied evenly, as he adjusted the collar on the sheepskin coat. "I like her. A lot."

"I just don't understand why you had to meet someone online. Why not someone from around here? There are plenty of really nice girls in Marietta."

"Because I didn't meet her in Marietta. I met her online and we clicked."

"But why? She's not from Montana. She's not even like us—"

"What does that mean?" he interrupted roughly, temper flaring. "Not like us?"

His mother bit her lower lip and said nothing.

"And her name is Sophie," he added. "Sophie's wonderful. She's smart, educated, successful. She has a great career, comes from a three-generation farming family. She understands my values, and how much the ranch means to me."

"And she's going to give up her job and her family to come here? She's going to live here and be happy here?" His mom made a scoffing noise. "I don't think so."

Joe didn't bother to dignify his mother's response with an answer. Instead, he opened the door and walked out, but for the entire thirty-minute drive to town, her words played over and over in his head.

JOE WOULD BE arriving any minute but Sophie hastily changed her blouse, and then peeled off her jeans and stepped into a long skirt, and stepped back to examine her reflection in the mirror on the closet door. No. Not good. Quickly she stripped off the skirt and tugged her jeans back on, and then changed back to her original blouse.

This was so stupid.

She scooped her loose hair into a ponytail and tightened the elastic, and turned her head right, left, studied her profile and then with a shake of her head, pulled the elastic out and let her hair spill down her back.

She couldn't do this. Be whatever it was she thought he wanted. She shouldn't be trying so hard. She barely knew him. How could she possibly make herself into whatever it was he wanted?

On the plane, she'd had butterflies. On the plane, she'd felt anxiety. But her anxiety tonight was different. Her anxiety was deeper, her pulse faster, her heart thudding with the awareness that Joe was gorgeous, and masculine, and full of hard edges. He wasn't going to be a man that was easily managed. He wasn't going to be overtly charming like Leo. He was himself, and she wasn't going to change him or dress him up or make him into something she wanted. She would have to take him, or leave him, period.

Conversely, he'd just have to take her or leave her as well, and that should reassure her, but it didn't.

The truth was, she'd never felt so alone in her life. She'd never doubted herself so much, either.

She either needed to go home, or make Montana permanent. She couldn't do limbo. She wasn't good with limbo. To be fair, though, she wasn't in total limbo. Joe had texted her fifteen minutes ago that he was on his way. He should be arriving in fifteen minutes. He was on his way. He obviously wanted to see her. He wanted marriage. A wife. And he'd picked her. They both wanted more, and they were both determined to be practical.

She couldn't let the prospect of a dinner date throw her, because it wasn't a date-date. She didn't need approval. They were past that. They were onto the commitment stage.

Weren't they?

Sophie glanced in the mirror at her reflection, seeing the

mass of long dark hair, the brown eyes, the arched eyebrows, the long mascaraed lashes and pink glossed lips. Had she put too much makeup on? Was she trying too hard?

She felt like she was trying too hard. That bothered her.

Sophie reached for a tissue and blotted the lip gloss, removing most of it. There, better. Less shiny. Less sexual.

And just thinking sexual, made her think of sex, which made her think of sex with Joe and her stomach rolled and her pulse quickened.

Sex with Joe. She couldn't quite imagine it yet. He was all man, rugged as heck, and he wanted kids, which meant they would eventually sleep together. Have sex together.

Her stomach did another uncomfortable flip.

What would he look like naked? Would he be lean and sinewy, or muscular and ripped? She wondered if he had chest hair, or no hair. She wondered—she broke off, overwhelmed by all the unknowns.

They weren't going to bed today—they hadn't even had a first kiss. They hadn't even held hands. My goodness, things were moving too fast and too slow. No wonder she was so confused.

SOPHIE WAS DOWNSTAIRS on Bramble House's front steps when he arrived, her long hair in a loose side ponytail, her black coat belted at her small waist, highlighting her curvy shape. Joe parked and stepped out of the truck. "You look pretty," he said, approaching her.

"Thank you."

"Would you mind walking to dinner? It's only a couple blocks over."

"Sounds good."

They'd walked a half block before Sophie broke the silence. "How was it when you went back home yesterday? Did your mom or your grandfather have anything to say about me being here?"

He hesitated, before shrugging. "A bit."

She shot him a sideways glance. "I have a feeling it was more than a bit."

"I don't think my grandfather has a lot to say about it, but my mom finds it suspicious that I met you online. That we have developed this relationship online. It's foreign to her. But then she doesn't do any social media."

"Are any of your brothers on Tinder then?"

"Oh, they're all on Tinder. She just doesn't know about it."

One of Sophie's dark winged eyebrows arched higher. "What about you? Are you on it?"

"I tried it a couple years ago when my brothers insisted I try, but it wasn't for me. I'm not interested in hooking up. I'm in need of more than a hookup."

They crossed the street, which was quick and easy as there was no traffic. "Not many people in our culture would consider marrying without love," Sophie said as they reached the other side.

"I thought that, and then I had dozens of answers to my ad. I probably had more than fifty women answer the ad, and most were quite serious about it. There are a lot of women looking for marriage and family without having to put themselves out there on the dating scene."

"The dating scene is definitely not very appealing," she agreed.

He had nothing to add, so he didn't.

They walked another block, and the spire of St. James came into view. "That's our Anglican church," he said, pointing toward the church. "Our Catholic church is on the other side of town, a couple blocks from the Depot."

"The Depot's a restaurant now?"

"Microbrewery with a limited menu. It's good. I go there with my brothers when they're in town."

"Where do you go when they're not here?"

Joe hesitated, then shrugged. "I don't. I stay home."

"You don't go out at all?"

"No."

"You don't have any friends you meet for a drink?"

"No."

He saw her lips part, and then she closed them and said nothing more.

SOPHIE KEPT REPLAYING Joe's answers to her questions over

and over in her head during dinner at the Italian restaurant. The food was good, and they shared a bottle of red wine, but Joe was so quiet tonight she was finding it rather exhausting trying to carry a conversation, and yet they weren't familiar enough with each other for the silence to be comfortable.

At least, she wasn't comfortable with the silence. She wanted to know him. Wanted to know more about his family and his life on the ranch.

She most of all wanted to know what his mom was thinking about her being here in Marietta. "Is there something I could do to help your mom feel better about me being here?" she asked as the entree dishes were cleared and they were presented with the dessert menu.

"No. She just needs time," he said.

"How much time?"

"I don't know."

It wasn't the answer she wanted. "Do you think it would help if we spent some time together? I could come up there one day, bring lunch to her—"

"I don't think that's a good idea."

Sophie pushed the dessert menu away without looking at it. "Did you know she'd react like this to me?"

"No. I'm surprised, actually. She was close with my last girlfriend. That was a long time ago, but even then, she liked her, and enjoyed her company a lot. I thought she'd be pleased I'd finally brought a new girlfriend home."

New girlfriend. Well, that was something. Not quite as

permanent as fiancée or wife but better than nothing. "What did your mom and girlfriend do together?"

"They'd bake together, watch TV together—they both loved *American Idol*. They'd exchange books. Charity loved romances, and my mom used to read them, too, and they'd talk about what they were reading." Joe looked hopefully at her. "Do you read romances?"

"I don't," Sophie said. "I'm more of a romantic suspense-thriller person."

"What do you watch on TV?"

"Police procedural."

Joe looked a little discouraged. She felt more than a little discouraged, too. "I haven't done a lot of baking—that was more my sister's thing—but I'm happy to bake with her."

"She doesn't bake anymore, not with her arthritis."

"I see." Sophie battled down her frustration and focused on putting her worries into words. "I have a question, and I hope it won't be too blunt, but I just need to know, is our relationship contingent on her approval?"

"No."

His answer was fast and blunt, which should reassure her, but it didn't. Maybe if she hadn't been through so much with Leo, she could relax and have faith that everything would work out, but her faith remained in short supply. "But I'm in town until she's okay with me."

"You're in town so that I can spend time with you away from my family."

"But eventually I'll be there on the ranch, with you."

"Yes."

"And with your family."

"Yes."

"And eventually this is all going to be… okay?"

"Yes," he said. "It will be okay."

He'd hesitated for just a moment before answering her, but she noticed the hesitation. She felt that hesitation all the way through her. "I feel like I'm in a state of limbo," she said softly. "I'm not good with limbo."

"I'm sorry. This isn't what I expected. I'm struggling to be patient with them, and so if I find this hard, and it's my family, it has to be even more frustrating for you."

It was a good apology, a very decent apology. Her eyes burned and she balled her hands in her lap, wishing she felt warmer, safer. It had been so long since she'd recognized her life, never mind the world. Once upon a time, she'd had such faith in people. Things. God.

"What are you thinking?" he asked.

She lifted her shoulders, wondering if she should tell him the truth. But he deserved the truth. People always deserved the truth. Truth was as essential as air and sun. "I'm thinking that maybe I shouldn't be here. I'm thinking we don't really have a plan after all."

"But we do have a plan."

"Do we?" She searched his clear blue eyes, looking for a hint of indecisiveness. "You really still want to marry?"

"Yes."

"Even though your mom is not in favor of me being here?"

"My mom needs time to get used to the idea of you being in my life. But she's not going to come between us. That's not happening."

But his mom had already come between them.

Sophie glanced away, lower lip caught between her teeth. She wanted to believe him. She did. But she wasn't confident right now.

"You don't believe me," he said.

"I want to believe you. It's why I'm here."

He reached out, caught her chin and gently turned her face to him. "I will always tell you the truth. If nothing else, believe that."

He released her as the waiter returned to see if they wanted dessert. Sophie didn't, but Joe ordered a black cup of coffee.

"You can drink caffeine at night?" she asked, as the waiter disappeared.

He nodded. "I got used to it with all the driving we did late at night, and my mom has always drunk coffee at night. Bad habit, I suppose."

"There are worse sins."

His mouth quirked and then the faint smile faded. "Tell me what you consider to be the worst sins."

"Is this a question to check my knowledge of the Bible?"

"Nope. Not interested in Biblical sins. I want to know what really bothers Sophie Correia."

"Lying. Dishonesty."

"I take it you have no patience for cheaters."

"None," she agreed. "We only have one life. I don't want to spend it living a lie."

"Do you feel as if we're living a lie right now? Because my mom doesn't know you're here to marry me?"

She was surprised he was so perceptive. She hadn't even completely put the pieces together, but that might be one of the reasons she felt increasingly anxious. "That's a good question, and maybe. I mean, I know why we're not sharing our news right now, and I understand why we need to give everyone time, but it adds to the uncertainty, doesn't it?"

"It does, yes."

"But you're still committed?"

"We marry Thursday. Five days from now."

Five days. So soon. But that was what she wanted, Sophie reminded herself. She wanted the uncertainty to go. She wanted a commitment. Permanence. "Great. Thank you."

"Is there anything else I can do to reassure you? What do you need from me?" Joe asked.

She liked the question. She liked how direct Joe could be. It allowed her to give him a direct answer.

She shook her head. "I just want to be your wife." And then she blushed because it sounded so bold put like that, much less to this big tough man who rarely smiled and struck her as impossibly self-contained.

"Why are you here in Montana marrying a stranger, Sophie? How can that be the right thing for you?"

His question made her cheeks flame and her insides lurch.

She reached for her wineglass and took a quick sip. "I was engaged and it ended abruptly, and badly," she said, returning the wineglass to the table, "and I don't want any more long engagements. I don't want promises that mean nothing."

"Tell me about him."

"There's not much to say. He didn't love me after all, and he married someone else rather quickly after we broke up."

"And that's why you want to marry a stranger?"

It sounded so ridiculous put like that. "It's not marrying a stranger that has me here. Marrying a stranger is terrifying. I'm here because you've made it clear that you want a wife, and you're making a commitment. I liked that. I responded to that. I want a commitment from a man. I'm turning thirty late June and I want a big family. I want to be a mom soon."

Joe didn't speak for a moment. "But this fiancé of yours—"

"Ex-fiancé," she corrected.

"He hurt you pretty bad."

Her heart squeezed and she hated how it still felt as if she'd swallowed hot coals, and how they'd burned her inside out. "I trusted him, so yes."

"What's his name?"

"Does it matter?"

"I think it's easier calling him a name than ex-fiancé."

Her mouth was dry, and her pulse raced, and this wasn't the conversation she wanted, but it was the conversation they were having. "Leo."

"How long were you with Leo?"

"Too long for him to have done what he did," she said huskily. "I wasn't left at the altar, but pretty dang close. Just days before the wedding he changed his mind. My mom and I spent days cancelling everything, and letting the four hundred guests know. It was beyond awful." She looked up, her gaze locking with Joe's. "I vowed I would never go through that again. I would never do the big engagement, the big wedding, the big buildup… All for what? Nothing. I got to be the fiancée with the sparkling diamond ring. I got to plan the black-tie formal wedding. But in the end there was no groom. There was no wedding. There was no husband. And I felt so cheated. It broke my heart and I don't ever want to be in that situation again."

"You just want the husband."

"Yes." She nodded emphatically. "I want the vows, I want the commitment, and I want the life I never got to live. I want to be a wife, and mom—now. Not in three years, or five years. I've had a successful career. I've been a working girl. I've paid my own bills for the past seven years. I don't need a man to pay my bills; that's not why I want to get married. I want to get married because I have this awful ticking clock telling me I'm at the peak of my fertility and if I don't start having babies I'll run out of time. Because I don't just want one, I want three or four. Maybe more. I come from a big family and it makes sense to have a big family, especially if you have a farm or ranch. Kids are cheaper than farm hands." She smiled as she said it, because she'd said it ironically. Those were the words her dad used to say when he dragged them out for their morning chores at the diary.

"And while I want to be a mom, I don't want to be a single parent. I don't want to do it on my own. I want a husband and kids and you'd said that you wanted a wife and kids, and we have the same goals. Or I thought we did when I arrived."

"We do," he answered firmly, signaling for the bill.

Outside the restaurant, she buttoned her coat and was about to put her hands in her coat pockets when Joe reached for her right hand and pulled her close to his side. The heat of his hand immediately warmed her, sending tiny sparks of heat and sensation through her.

She glanced down at their hands and then up at his profile. "That's brave of you," she murmured.

His fingers tightened and then eased. "What do you mean?"

"Just that I was beginning to wonder if you were afraid

of me."

Joe's laugh rumbled low and rough. "You're little. You barely reach my shoulder. Definitely not afraid of you."

That husky note in his voice, coupled with the warmth of his hand, made her feel things, new things. It also made her strangely daring. "Just afraid of touching me then?" she teased.

He stopped walking and turned to face her, her hand still firmly linked with his. "I was being respectful."

"Glad we're past that. I was beginning to think you might be..." Her shoulders twisted.

"You don't think I like women?"

"*No.* I was thinking maybe you weren't interested in *me.*"

"Because I'm being respectful?"

"I get it if you're not attracted to me—"

"Not the case."

"Chemistry's a tricky thing. It's either there, or it's not."

He barked out a laugh, but he didn't sound amused. He drew her closer to his big body. "Chemistry, or lack of it, isn't the issue there."

"Then what is the issue?"

"You want to have this talk on Church Street?"

"No one's looking. No one's paying us the least bit of attention."

"They would if I kissed you."

Her pulse leaped in her veins and for a second she felt tingly from head to toe. "At least I'd have a first kiss."

He gave her a considering look. "Are you complaining?"

"Just worried. And letting you know I'm worried. I can't see marrying someone that's not at all physically attracted to me."

"Oh, I'm attracted. That's not an issue. I've just been holding back, being chivalrous. It wouldn't do to bring you out here and immediately jump your bones. Can't see that inspiring much trust."

She liked the energy crackling through him, and how it made her come alive. He was impressively warm and real and energy surged through her, little zings of sensation and pleasure. "But what if once you kiss me, you don't like kissing me?"

"Then I'll teach you how I like to kiss."

"Can kissing be taught?"

"Everything can be taught."

There was something sexy and dangerous in his tone, and another hot ripple of sensation washed through her. Things were beginning to get interesting. She liked it. Maybe too much. "You've had experience, then? You're not a virgin."

Heat flared in his eyes. "Not a virgin, sorry. You?"

The warmth between them practically crackled and burned. Her body felt hot, her skin felt sensitive, her pulse was thumping. She'd been waiting for this, waiting for something to make her want to be here... want to be with him. "Not a virgin, either. Hope that isn't an issue for you."

"I'm glad you're not a virgin. I've no need to be someone's first." His gaze locked with hers, and held. "I'm more interested in being your last. When we marry, there's not going to be anyone else for me, and I'm not going to be okay with you having anyone else—"

"I wouldn't. I'm not a cheater. I'd never do that to you."

"Not even if you were lonely and unhappy on the ranch?"

"I'd tell you I was lonely. I'd tell you I was unhappy. And I'd hope we could figure out our difficulties together." She looked up into his face, looking intently into his pale blue eyes. "But that's a long way away since we haven't even made it to first base."

"Is that what you need? If that's the case, let's not leave you wanting." Joe pulled her all the way against him, his arm dropping low around her waist to hold her securely to his chest. His head dipped, and his mouth brushed her cheekbone and then lower near the corner of her lips. "Can't have you wanting for anything." And then his mouth covered hers, and the kiss was hard, and demanding, and more than a little possessive. He kissed her as if she was his, and only his, and he, and only he, knew how to kiss her.

Shockingly, he knew how to kiss her. With heat, and desire, and more than a little expertise. She shuddered as his lips moved over hers, parting hers, to taste and tease the inside of her mouth. She shuddered again as his hand wound through her long hair, sliding through the strands until she felt his palm at the base of her neck. The press of his fingers against her nape made the air catch in her throat and for a moment she forgot to breathe. His touch was a maddening pleasure and she couldn't stifle her breathless sighs.

By the time he lifted his head, she was a mass of quivering nerves. She stared up at him unable to think of a single coherent thing to say.

"Feel better?" he asked, his eyes dark like denim, his deep voice pitched even lower, the sound a sexy, husky rasp that scraped her sense and made her knees go weak.

"Depends on your definition of better," she answered, voice equally husky. It had been an amazing kiss. Dazzling, dizzying. She still craved more. "I certainly feel different."

"Different how?"

"Different as in wow, cowboy, you do that so well."

His blue gaze locked with hers, his expression so warm, so intimate she felt as if she'd go up in flames any second.

"Why are you still single?" he asked.

The question made her eyes sting and her chest ache. The breeze caught at her long hair, making it swirl around her face. She tucked a strand back, behind her ear. "Spent too long with the wrong one."

"He must have been blind and stupid."

Her lower lip quivered as he drew a reluctant smile from her. "Or maybe I was the stupid one, loving someone who didn't love me back."

He reached out to catch a long tendril of her hair, peeling it off her eyelashes and smoothing it back. "Is that why you answered my ad? Your heart took a beating and you gave up on love?"

"Something like that."

"I feel like there's more to the story than you're telling me."

"Maybe," she admitted.

"You want to tell me?"

She glanced around, her gaze sweeping the deserted block, before she looked back at him. "Standing here on Church Street? No, thank you."

He smiled crookedly, aware she'd just handed him his own words. "There's nobody here."

"Maybe not, but this is a story that requires tequila. Lots of it."

"Let's go get drunk."

She blushed, laughed, and gave her head a firm shake. "Nope. That's not happening."

"Why not? I'm off the rest of the night, with nothing to do until tomorrow morning."

"Exactly the problem. If I drink with you, cowboy, we're going to end up in bed."

His blue gaze heated. "Is that a bad thing?"

Heat washed through her. He wasn't the iceman she'd painted him to be and the energy between them was dangerously electric at the moment. "It is if we're not married." She tried to keep her tone light but a husky note entered her voice and she liked the warmth in her veins, liked the way it felt to feel something, but she didn't trust it. Maybe that was the biggest problem. She simply didn't trust anyone or anything right now. "If we marry, you get all of me. But until we do that, I'm not sleeping with you, no matter how tempting it seems."

"*If* we marry?"

Her gaze met his in the dark and held. She searched his eyes, searching for truth, for sincerity. "A lot of things seem up in the air right now, don't you think?"

"Things might not be smooth sailing at the Wyatt ranch, but nothing's in the air. This time next week, you'll be Mrs. Joseph Wyatt."

Chapter Four

JOE DROVE BACK to the ranch in a frustrating state of arousal. He'd forgotten what it felt like to actually physically want someone and he desired Sophie. She was beautiful, feminine, smart, interesting. But he also felt a strong need to protect her, and that need was problematic because he couldn't protect her from the rigors of life on the ranch, and he couldn't protect her from the loneliness that came from living on the ranch. Being a rancher's wife required a lot of sacrifices and he was worried Sophie wasn't tough enough for his life.

He worried she wouldn't be able to handle his mother's rejection, if the rejection continued.

He'd have some hard words with his mother if she continued to be so cold toward Sophie, and he dreaded that. His mother had been widowed young with four small boys and she'd never once tried to replace his dad. She'd poured herself into being the best mom she could, and she'd been a great one, a singularly devoted mom. In his heart, he believed his mom would come around. She'd eventually warm to Sophie. Sophie just needed to not lose faith.

Impulsively, Joe called Sophie as he neared the ranch. She answered after two rings.

"I didn't wake you, did I?" he asked, wondering.

"Just in bed watching a show on my laptop," she said, her voice warm. "Are you home already?"

"Not yet," he answered, distracted as he pictured her in bed. What was she wearing? Did she sleep naked, or wear real pajamas? And just like that, his body hardened. "Want me to call back?"

"No. You're immensely more interesting."

His pulse thumped, and his body hummed, and he very much wanted to get her alone. He very much wanted to have her all to himself. "Your program can't be that entertaining then."

She let out a gurgle of a laugh. "So, what's up?"

"I'd be a fool not to realize you're getting the short end of the stick. After we marry we're not going to be living in town. Any friends you make will be a good thirty-minute drive away. You're going to feel isolated at the ranch, and if my mom and granddad don't come around, maybe miserable—"

"Okay, let's stop there. Your mom isn't going to make me miserable. Your mom just doesn't know me yet, and when she does, and she realizes I'm not about to come between you two, she'll like me. A lot. Your grandfather isn't going to make me miserable, either. He's not that kind of guy. He's just reserved. Over time, he'll mellow, and when we have our first baby, he'll melt."

"I just wish they were a bit more welcoming."

"It's fine, Joe, it is. I almost think it's better to not wear rose-colored glasses going into this thing. We're smart to be realistic. We're mature adults. We don't need a fairy tale."

"But a little romance wouldn't hurt. I think it's time I took you out to a movie or maybe dancing."

"We don't have to go dancing," she said quickly. "I'd actually just be happy having dinner with your family."

It was the last thing he'd thought she'd say and he had no answer for that.

Sophie added, "I think it's important we try to include them. It'll be my fourth night here and I've only seen your mom that first night and it wasn't a good first meet." She hesitated. "I understand she might need time to get used to me, but she won't get to know me if she and I are kept apart, and I worry about trying to move to the ranch with her not happy that I'm there."

"Tomorrow might not work. Mom has a ladies' birthday group luncheon tomorrow in town, and usually comes home exhausted. What if we try for the night after? Monday night? It'll give me a chance to run the idea past her."

AFTER HANGING UP, Sophie crawled under her covers and pulled the comforter up to her chin. She'd been glad to hear Joe's voice but he was distinctly unenthusiastic about getting

Sophie and his mom together for dinner again. The lack of enthusiasm put an ache in her chest. She'd left a hard situation at home and it hadn't crossed her mind that she might not be welcome on the Wyatt ranch. For some foolish reason she'd built the Wyatts into this family who'd want her, and love her. Instead they didn't want her.

What if they never warmed to her?

What if there was always tension between Mrs. Wyatt and herself?

Sophie squeezed her eyes shut, unable to bear the thought. Until this falling out with Sarah, Sophie had always been close to her family. She was someone that loved family, and needed family.

She'd just have to win Mrs. Wyatt over. She didn't know how, but as Sophie drifted to sleep, she told herself she was up for the challenge.

But the next morning, when Joe phoned, he didn't have good news. He said it was unlikely he'd see her for dinner due to his mom's afternoon event, and she'd need some extra care after returning from town, but he could come in after dinner and they could go get a drink or dessert someplace.

"Sounds good," she answered. "Call me when you leave your place."

Joe did call when he was pulling away from the house, and Sophie told him to just drive to the bed-and-breakfast, park, and come in. "I've picked up some dessert, and can make coffee here. We'll have pie in my room, if that's okay."

"Sounds good to me. See you in thirty."

He was there in precisely thirty, and Sophie was waiting downstairs on Bramble's front porch for him when he arrived. She watched as he parked his truck and then headed up the walkway.

She smiled as his boots thudded on the wooden steps. "Welcome."

"I feel like I haven't seen you in forever," he said.

"I know. I feel the same."

"How did you stay busy today?"

"I walked a lot," she admitted, gesturing for him to follow.

She could feel him behind her as they climbed the stairs, his energy electric as always. He was so very male, and so physical and she found herself again wondering what it would be like to make love to him, and then she immediately panicked, because she wasn't ready for that. She wanted to know Joe, and she wanted to kiss him, but there was this part of her that desperately needed to take it slow.

Her heart craved love and affection, but her mind told her not to trust anyone. But Sophie couldn't very well show up in Montana and keep Joe at arm's length. He was expecting a wife. She'd agreed to be that wife. If only she had more confidence in herself… and him.

Inside her room she closed the door and her room suddenly seemed very small indeed. "You remember this room," she said a little breathlessly.

His gaze swept the room. He nodded. "I do."

"Nothing's changed," she said brightly. "I haven't broken anything yet, either."

The corner of his mouth lifted in amusement. Creases fanned from his light blue eyes. "That's good. You know, it never crossed my mind if I should ask you if you were clumsy."

"I'm not. You should be reassured."

"I am. Thank you." His smile deepened. "You're nervous."

"You already know me so well."

Joe laughed, but the sound was husky and sexy and kind. "Why are you nervous?"

"I'm not sure. Maybe it's because I get excited to see you, and then I realize this is all so new and it's rather weird—"

"It is at that," he agreed.

"Is it too weird?" she asked, brow creasing, anxiety making her voice rise a little higher than she would have liked.

"Depends if you think a mail-order bride is strange."

Sophie's heart raced, and she realized her heart wasn't racing out of fear, but adrenaline, and awareness, as well as a whisper of desire. Just by being in her room, Joe was turning her little haven into a physically charged space. He wasn't even standing particularly close to her, but he radiated a potent masculine energy that made her tingle. Joe Wyatt was one rugged, handsome, appealing man.

Now if he'd just kiss her.

"It's a little strange," she whispered. "But as mail-order grooms go, you're not bad." She dampened her dry upper lip with her tongue. "You have all your teeth and a good head of hair. I really can't complain."

His lips curved, and a glint shone in his eyes. "You're getting yourself really wound up right now, aren't you?"

"Yes."

"Why?"

"I don't know." She took a deep breath. "Maybe you should just kiss me."

"Maybe I should." Joe closed the distance between them, and wrapped an arm low around her waist, bringing her up against him. Heat flickered in his eyes and then his head dropped, his mouth covering hers.

Just the brush of his mouth on hers sent darts of sensation throughout her. This kiss was different from the others. This kiss felt hungry and familiar and it stole her breath, making her head spin. Sophie melted against him, her arms wrapping around his lean waist, needing more, not less. Craving pressure, comfort, pleasure. After being so nervous, it was a relief to discover that the desire was real. There was relief in the heat and hunger.

By the time Joe lifted his head, she felt boneless and Sophie leaned weakly against his chest, vision cloudy, senses stirred. "That's some kiss," she murmured, still unable to focus.

"And that's just hello," he answered, cupping her face

and kissing her once more, before letting her go. "I think you better distract me with some pie, or I'm going to find it hard to keep my hands off of you."

"Pie it is, then," she said, cheeks hot, body tingling, because as delicious as the kiss was, that's all she was ready for. It didn't worry her. They were still such a new couple, they were still getting to know each other.

But as she served the pie on the paper plates she'd bought downtown, Sophie pressed her lips together, her mouth swollen and sensitive.

He did kiss well. He kissed the way she'd always wanted to be kissed.

Did that mean he'd make love to her the same way?

Pushing the thought away, Sophie handed Joe his pie, and poured him coffee, and climbed on the bed. Joe sat next to her on the bed, side by side, backs to the antique headboard. Sophie kept stealing glances at Joe as he made quick work on his apple crumble pie. "I'm sorry there's no ice cream," she said.

"I like it this way," he answered. "Ice cream makes the crust soggy."

"I agree with you." She stabbed into the crust and broke off a big chunk. "Hope you didn't mind not going out. I kind of wanted you all to myself."

His fork paused midair. His voice dropped, deepening. "You'll give a man ideas, talking like that."

She blushed and gave his big shoulder—which was also

very warm—a little push. "So when was your last girlfriend? Has it really been a while?"

"Years."

"What about casual hookups?"

"It's been a while for that, too."

"Why?"

"Marietta's a small town. I don't want everyone knowing my business."

"You think people would talk?"

"I know they'd talk."

She ate a bite of pie, chewing slowly, thinking about what he'd said. She, too, came from a small town, although it wasn't as small as Marietta, and yes, people gossiped, but they gossiped everywhere, and why did it matter what people thought? "Do people's opinions matter so much?" she asked, when she could.

"I'm just private. I'm not comfortable with lots of attention."

"Have you always been that way?"

"Hard to say. Maybe not. A lot of things changed when my dad died." He hesitated, then added flatly, "Everything changed. So I'm sure I changed."

"How old were you when he died?"

"Seven."

"That's so young. I'm so sorry." She looked at Joe but his features were hard, his expression shuttered. "Do you mind me asking, how did he die?"

"Car accident."

Sophie waited for him to say more, but he didn't. Instead, he set his half-eaten pie on the nightstand, clearly done with it. She looked at his half-eaten slice of pie and felt bad. She hadn't meant to ruin their time together. They had so little time together.

"I'm sorry," she said, setting the remains of her pie slice on her nightstand. "I shouldn't have pushed."

"You didn't," he said gruffly. "It's just not easy to talk about. Mom never really got over losing him, and Granddad, well, he lost both his sons in the accident, and I don't know if that kind of grief ever goes away." Joe looked at her, expression strained. "My dad and his brother Sam—"

"Your uncle was named Sam?"

"Yeah. I was named after my dad, Joseph, and my brother Sam was named after my dad's best friend, his brother."

"That's sweet."

"Yeah, well, the rest of the story isn't sweet. It's pretty awful. My dad and Uncle Sam were on the way to a rodeo in Cheyenne when they were killed, taken out by a tractor trailer. They died together. Probably instantly. Mom fell apart when she heard. Can't blame her. She was just twenty-seven with four little boys all under the age of eight, so Granddad drove over to where we were living in Northern California, scooped us all up, and moved us in with him on the ranch. He's taken care of us ever since."

"Your grandfather is a good man."

"He's old school. Granddad isn't a big talker, but he shows up and does what's needed to be done."

Sophie turned on her hip to face Joe. "Is that why you decided to get married now? Because it's what needs to be done?"

Joe reached out and lifted a long dark tendril of her hair and wrapped it around his fingers. "It's time there was another generation on that ranch. It's a big place, a lot of land. The house needs family… kids." He tugged gently on her hair. "I need family. Kids. It's not the same with my brothers gone."

"You find it lonely."

He hesitated. "I do."

"Hopefully we can change that."

"I like that use of we," he said, leaning over her, his mouth brushing hers. "It sounds good."

That brief kiss made her pulse jump and her heart beat double-time. Joe's kiss was pure electricity. "We have to be a team," she said, fingertips brushing his hard angled jaw, feeling the rasp of his day-old beard. "We have to stick together, and not let friends or family divide us."

"You think my mom will divide us?"

The man was quick, she'd give him that. Sophie chose her words carefully. "Not just your mom, my family, too. What we're doing—getting married after meeting on the internet—is crazy, and they'll think we're crazy."

"Maybe we are," he said, before his mouth claimed hers

again.

Sophie shivered against him, the tantalizing pressure of his mouth sending fresh licks of fire up and down on her spine. She reached out and caught his shirt, tugging on the fabric, pulling him closer, and he responded in kind, deepening the kiss, his mouth taking hers with heat and possession. Sophie lost track of time as the delicious kiss went on and on.

When Joe finally lifted his head, his blue eyes sparked with fire. "You have no idea how much I like kissing you," he growled. "Your mouth was made for me."

She warmed from the inside out. "Yeah?"

"Yeah." He kissed her once more, before rising from the bed. "How many kids did you say you wanted again?"

"Four. Five?"

"I was hoping that's what you'd said." He walked to the chair and reached into his coat, pulling out a small ring box and popping the lid open; he looked her straight in the eye. "Sophie Correia, marry me. Let's get that big family started."

She blushed and looked from his intensely blue eyes to the dazzling diamond and then back up into his beautiful eyes. Her heart beat double time as she answered, "Yes, I will, Joe Wyatt."

She bit her lip, nervous, and excited, as he slipped the stunning diamond ring onto her finger. It was a simple platinum band with a large diamond solitaire.

He adjusted the band on her finger, making sure the brilliant diamond was facing up. "How does it feel?"

"Perfect."

"If you'd rather pick out a different ring—"

"No, it's really perfect. I love the simplicity of the design. It's elegant and the diamond is so sparkly." She felt a rush of emotion. This was all suddenly very real. "So, we're marrying this Thursday."

"Or sooner."

Her eyebrows shot up.

"Why not?" he said. "We'll have dinner at my place tomorrow night, show off your new ring, and get married the next day."

She exhaled in a rush. This was most definitely getting real. "Okay."

He looked at her steadily. "You're not sure."

"I… no… that's not true. I'm sure about us." She bit into her lower lip, thinking about dinner tomorrow night. "I just don't know how they will feel when we announce our news. But maybe there won't be any easy way to break the news."

"We could just start with the engagement," he said.

"And hide the part about us getting married the next day?"

"I wasn't going to invite them to the ceremony at the courthouse."

"I don't want to deceive them. I hate dishonesty."

"I do, too, but I'm beginning to think the best thing to

do is tell them after, so there isn't a lot of drama ahead of time. Unless you enjoy drama…"

She laughed. No, she most definitely did not enjoy drama. She'd left California to escape drama. "It's going to be challenging either way, isn't it?"

"Yes." He leaned forward, kissed her forehead. "The drama will pass. Things will settle. It'll get easier." He smiled sympathetically. "But first it's going to get harder."

"Great," she muttered.

"So tomorrow, for dinner, what sounds good?"

"How about I make dinner and bring it up with me? That way there is no fuss at your end."

"That's a lot of work."

"Joe, I have nothing to do all day. I need a purpose."

"Do you miss working?"

"I do, actually. I've always worked." She glanced down at the big sparkly white diamond on her finger. It was truly gorgeous. "I've been thinking about looking for a part-time or temporary job. Not sure how you'd feel about it, but I'm not used to not working, and it'd help make time pass faster." She paused and looked up at him, trying to gauge Joe's reaction. "Would you mind me getting a job here in town?"

"No. But what happens after you move to the ranch?"

"I'd like to keep working if I could. Obviously, once we have kids that would change things, but until we do, I wouldn't mind driving from the ranch into town. I'm used to driving."

"It's a hard drive in bad weather."

"I'm a careful driver. I don't take unnecessary risks. I just need to ship my car out from California, but I could do that soon."

"Is your car four-wheel drive?" he asked.

"No. It's a little Prius. Gets great gas mileage."

"Which might work for the summer, but not our winter. Roads up where we are can be treacherous with a hard rain."

"I can also sell my car and buy something here. My sister-in-law's family has a car dealership in Tulare. I'm sure they'd sell it for me."

"That would probably be the best way to go. There's no point trying to get your car here, just to sell it. We'll look for a car for you for here. But for tomorrow, I'll pick you up."

"Sounds good. I was thinking I'd make lasagna. I know we just had Italian the other night but I make a pretty mean lasagna if your family likes it."

"Granddad loves lasagna and he doesn't get it very often, but where would you make it?"

"I'm going to ask Eliza if I could use the kitchen here at Bramble House. She might say no, but she might say yes. If she says no, I'll just pick up something at Rocco's that I can bring with me."

"Sounds great. I'll be here tomorrow at five."

THE NEXT MORNING Sophie walked to the grocery store to buy the groceries needed to make dinner, and then returned to Bramble to make her homemade red sauce. She ended up making two large lasagnas, one to be eaten tonight, and the other to be put in the Wyatts' freezer for another night. As she layered the red sauce and noodles and cheese, she kept glancing down at her diamond ring, distracted by the sparkling stone on her finger.

She was officially engaged. They'd be marrying tomorrow. Things were moving fast now.

Joe was there a few minutes before five to pick her up, and he helped her carry all the dinner items to his truck, where the lasagnas went on the floor of the back of his cab.

At the ranch house, she turned on the oven and put one lasagna in to reheat, and then halfway through, added the loaf of garlic bread. She tossed the salad as everything warmed.

"You look pretty cute in my kitchen," Joe said, entering through the back door. He'd been in the barn checking on the horses and as he hung up his coat and set his hat upside down on the narrow table, Sophie's heart turned over. It was suddenly so very domestic, and it crossed her mind that this was what it'd be like when she lived here. She'd be busy prepping dinner and he'd come in and hopefully he'd always smile at her as if she was rather irresistible.

She smiled at him, pleased and yet also shy. "Do I?"

"You do." He went to the sink and washed his hands.

"You make me hungry."

"Must be the garlic bread."

"Hmmm. No, it's you. Hard to explain, but it feels right seeing you in here. You kind of light everything up and make the room feel good."

It was probably one of the nicest things she'd ever heard and for a split second her eyes burned and a lump filled her throat. "You just made my day, Joe Wyatt."

He reached for a dish towel and dried his hands. "Granddad told me that Mom is hoping to talk to you. Do we have time before dinner?"

"We're probably ten minutes away from eating. But I could also let everything sit a bit. It won't hurt the lasagna if it sits awhile before we serve." Sophie hesitated. "Do you know what she wants to talk to me about?"

Joe shook his head.

"Do you think she knows about the engagement?" Sophie asked.

"I haven't told her, and you're not wearing the ring," he said.

She patted the pocket of her jeans. "It's right here. I was going to put it on when we share the news. Should I put it on now?"

"No." He put his hands on his lean hips and looked toward the dining room and family room beyond. "I don't know what she's going to say. I'm kind of worried."

"Whatever it is, I'll survive."

He growled his displeasure. "I hate this."

"It's just a phase, right?"

"I admire you, Sophie. You look delicate but you're pretty dang tough."

"I told you, I'm a farmer's daughter." She went to him, put her hands on his chest, and stood up on tiptoe. "Kiss me for luck."

He did. He kissed her as if she was his, and only his, his tongue teasing the seam of her lips, before stroking inside her mouth, making her body warm and melt. Kissing him always made her want more, and the more promised to be unbearably good.

She was breathing hard when she stepped back. "Wow. Kissing you is like the Fourth of July. Fireworks every single time."

He laughed, softly, appreciatively, and gave her butt a pat as she headed for the family room. "Shout if you need me."

"Ha. Just don't let the lasagna burn. It needs to come out in ten. I've already taken the foil off."

"Setting the timer now," he answered. "But brace yourself; I have a feeling she's going to ask you a million questions."

"That's okay."

"They might be uncomfortable questions," he added as she reached the swinging door.

Sophie turned, glanced back at him. "What makes you

say that?"

"Because she spent the morning asking me a lot of un-comfortable questions."

"Ah."

"Want to put off the interrogation?"

She squared her shoulders, shook her head. "Nope. Let's do this."

A million uncomfortable questions, Sophie repeated to herself, as she made her way down the hall and into the small paneled family room where the TV had already been muted in anticipation of Sophie's arrival. "Hi," Sophie said, as she entered the room. "Am I interrupting anything?"

Mrs. Wyatt gestured for her to sit, her hand waving to the upholstered sofa opposite her armchair. "Joe said you'd made dinner tonight."

"Yes, lasagna. I hope you like lasagna."

"Haven't had it in years."

"It's my mom's recipe." Sophie sat down, and smoothed her emerald-green blouse over her hips. "She's a good cook. At least, we all think so."

"She's still alive?"

Sophie nodded. "She lives on our dairy farm in Tulare."

"Is that where you still live? Tulare?"

"Actually, I was an hour north. Just outside of Kings-burg."

"Why there?"

"I worked for Brazer Farms and they were headquartered

there."

"What did you do?"

"Import and exports."

"You met Joe online," Mrs. Wyatt said, abruptly changing the direction of the conversation.

Sophie refused to let herself be rattled. "Yes."

"Why go online to meet a man?"

"I work long hours, and I'm not the type to go hang out in bars."

"Why Joe? What made him the one?"

Joe's mom would need a good answer. "Joe is solid," she said, choosing her words with care. "He's honest. I admire his integrity."

"That's it? Nothing about his body or his good looks?"

Sophie's face heated. "Do you want me to tell you he's hot? That I think he's gorgeous and has an incredible body?"

"I'd find it more believable. Integrity and honesty are hard to measure over the internet."

"I liked his photo. He has a great face, a strong face. I found his profile appealing."

"What did he say in his profile? I asked him to show me this dating app but he said you have to be a member. That made me suspicious. And so I'm trying to figure out why someone like you, would be here."

"You mentioned Joe's looks, and yes, he's easy on the eyes, but I liked that he was a rancher. I liked that he made it clear that he was committed to his Montana ranch and his

family. I liked that he was upfront about what he wanted—
he wants to marry and have a family, and he plans to raise his
kids here on his property. He made it clear that he's not
looking to move, and he's not wanting a city lifestyle. He
wants his children where he was raised."

"That didn't strike you as awfully one-sided to you?"

"It struck me as real. Truthful. I'd far rather a man tell
me his limitations than pretend he's open to all kinds of
things, when it's not true."

"Life on a ranch is hard. Joe will always spend more time
with the land, than with you."

"My dad was up at four thirty every morning to milk the
cows, and was in bed early after the evening milking. There
weren't a lot of vacations because he couldn't leave the cows,
or the milking, to anyone else."

"Your mom didn't mind?"

"My mom viewed herself as his business partner. She
knew when she married him that it was a family dairy. She
knew that Dad had been raised in that house and that once
he married, he'd raise his kids in the same house. If I was a
boy, my kids would be growing up on the same property,
too."

"So your grandparents shared the same house?"

"They built another house on the property for themselves. After she was done raising kids, Grandma wanted
something a little nicer, with more creature comforts, so
Grandpa built her a custom house giving her everything she

ever wanted."

Mrs. Wyatt studied Sophie for a long moment. "We don't have a fancy house. We don't have anything modern. Joe wants to build something for himself one day, at least, that's always been his plan, but he hasn't even started. If you end up with him, you're going to be living with me and his grandfather, and then when Joe's brothers come home, they fill the place up. You won't have a lot of privacy."

"I didn't have a lot of privacy growing up. There were five of us kids."

"So why aren't you there now?"

Mrs. Wyatt was relentless, but Sophie wasn't going to be intimidated. "Because you don't take a dairy and divide it five ways. We always knew my oldest brother John would take over from my dad, and he has. My brother Michael works with him, too, but my other brother has become a lawyer. My sister"—Sophie broke off and drew a breath—"she just recently married and is enjoying being a newlywed."

"What does she do?"

"She was a preschool teacher for a couple years but isn't working right now."

"Did you like your job?"

"I did."

"Do you still have it?"

"I'm taking a break from it. But they'd hired me back if I wanted to return."

"You quit your job to come here?"

"I was already looking for something else."

"Why?"

"I'd been there since college. Change is good."

Summer reached for her cane, bringing it closer to her legs. "California dairy folks are Portuguese or Dutch. I take it you're from a Portuguese family."

"I am."

"This fruit farm, fruit company, you worked for, were they also Portuguese?"

Sophie hid her surprise. "Yes."

"Will it be a problem for your family that Joe isn't Portuguese?"

"No." Sophie saw Mrs. Wyatt's expression, and she shook her head firmly. "When I marry, it's going to be someone that's right for me, not necessarily right for my family."

Mrs. Wyatt's eyebrows lifted but, before she could say anything, Joe appeared. "Dinner is ready and on the table," he said. "Come eat before it's cold."

Joe helped his mom to her feet and escorted her to her chair before pulling out Sophie's chair at the dining room table. "You survived the inquisition?" he asked under his breath as she sat down.

"Everything is fine," she reassured him. "But will it be when we tell them about the engagement?"

"Leave it to me," he answered. "I'll bring it up when I think the time is right, I promise."

He kept his word. They got through dinner with Joe and his grandfather doing most of the talking, discussing weather and if the predicted storm would really come to pass.

Sophie could barely eat, though, thinking about their announcement and wondering how his grandfather and mother would respond. But finally dinner was over and Joe poured cups of coffee and they were sitting at the table when Joe bluntly announced that he and Sophie were engaged.

"I asked her to marry me Sunday night, and she said yes," he added. "We're not interested in a long engagement, either." He looked at Sophie. "Have you shown them your ring?"

"No, but I'd love to," she said, shyly drawing the ring from her pocket and sliding it on her finger. She turned her hand around so they could see the flash of fire in the diamond. "It's a beautiful ring."

For a moment, there was stunned silence and then Mrs. Wyatt asked, "Do your brothers know?"

"No, you're the first we've told," Joe answered, which was true.

Silence stretched and then Melvin Wyatt got to his feet, came around the table, and kissed Sophie on the cheek. "Congratulations," he said. "Looking forward to having you join the family." He stopped by Joe's chair, and clasped him on the shoulder before stepping out of the room.

Sophie felt strangely moved by Melvin Wyatt's congratulations and kiss. It was kind, and it felt sincere. Mrs. Wyatt on the other hand looked as if she'd been turned to stone.

Her expression was completely frozen.

Mrs. Wyatt finally spoke. "You two barely know each other."

"It just feels right, Mom," Joe answered, reaching out to cover Sophie's hand with his. "And I know it's going to be a change having Sophie here, but it will be a good change."

Mrs. Wyatt's brow lowered and her gaze rested for a long moment on Sophie before she sighed. "We will see, won't we?"

JOE MADE SOPHIE a cup of peppermint tea and told her to take a seat at the kitchen table while he cleaned up. "I'd feel guilty watching you work," she protested.

He pulled out a chair for her, and stood there until she took it. "No need to feel guilty if you're keeping me company. Usually, I'm in here on my own."

"Do you always do the dishes?" she asked as he quickly, efficiently, scraped and washed.

"Yes."

"Even though you cook?"

He covered the remaining lasagna with foil and put it in the fridge. "Yes."

She propped her elbows on the table. "What about the nights you meet me for dinner?"

"I make dinner before I go."

She blinked, shocked. "*Every* time?"

"It's easier for them."

"And harder for you."

He shrugged. "I'm not going to make more work for my mom and grandfather."

"I had no idea."

"I've enjoyed our dinners out. I get tired of my own cooking." He quickly buffed the silverware dry and put those away as well. "And your lasagna was fantastic. Better than Rocco's."

"That's nice of you to say, but not true."

"Take a compliment, Sophie. Let me be impressed."

She glanced around the tidied kitchen. Joe had made very quick work with cleanup. "I'm the one that's impressed by you. You work all day outside and then come in and take care of everything inside, too."

"I don't want to talk about me." He closed the distance between them, pulled her from her chair so that he could sit down in it, before drawing her down on his lap. "Much better," he said.

Sophie's pulse raced. Air seemed to catch in her throat. Being this close to Joe was almost overwhelming. Energy crackled around him. Awareness sizzled between them.

Her gaze traveled up, over his broad chest, wide shoulders, to his hard jaw and very firm lips. "What do you want to talk about then?" she asked, sounding breathless to her own ears.

"You."

"I don't want to talk about me," she answered huskily.

"Then maybe we just don't talk," he said, dipping his head and capturing her mouth with his.

She felt right in his arms, Joe thought, his hand on Sophie's hip, sliding up her back, bringing her even closer so that her full soft breasts pressed against his chest. He could smell a vanilla scent and wasn't sure if it was her skin or her hair but it made him feel even hungrier.

It had been forever since he'd felt this alive, this carnal.

She felt right on his lap, in this kitchen, in this house. In his life.

He broke the kiss off to look at her, wanting to see her, this woman who would soon be his wife.

Her cheeks had darkened, the soft skin flushed pink. Her eyes had darkened, too, but this close, he could see the brown irises were flecked with bright bits of gold. Her lips were slightly swollen. She was breathing hard. He could see the little pulse race at the base of her throat. He dropped his head, kissed her there, and then scraped his teeth along the side of her neck.

She whimpered and arched against him. The helpless shift of her hips made him nearly groan. It had been years since he'd been with anyone and suddenly his control was being tested.

A sharp rap came from the door to the dining room. Joe looked up. His mom stood in the doorway, leaning on her cane. "Billy just called. They were hoping to come home next weekend for Easter but it's not going to work out after all. Not sure about Sam."

Sophie had tried to jump off his lap, but Joe wouldn't let her go. "I'll give Billy a call after I drop Sophie off."

His mom's lips thinned but she said nothing else, just turned around and slowly walked out.

Sophie sat stiffly in his arms after his mom left the kitchen. "Maybe it's time you took me back," she whispered.

"You're fine here."

She drew a ragged breath. "If it's okay with you, I think I'd rather go."

CHAPTER FIVE

THEY DIDN'T END up getting married on Tuesday as they'd planned because early Tuesday morning while heading to the barn Joe's grandfather slipped on a patch of black ice, and went down face first, bruising his temple and slicing up his cheekbone, requiring a couple of stitches. Fortunately, Granddad didn't like to be fussed over and after taking it slow the rest of Tuesday he just wanted to get back to work on Wednesday, telling Joe to stop hovering over him like an old woman.

It was all Joe could do to not roll his eyes. "I'm not hovering," he said to his grandfather. "I'm just wanting you to not do too much today. I'm supposed to head into Marietta—"

"Then go."

"But I can put it off another day, if I'm needed here."

His grandfather snorted. "You're not needed here. I might be eighty-two but I'm not in need of a nursemaid."

"I don't even know what a nursemaid is, Granddad."

"Maybe you should read more."

Joe grinned. "I think you're feeling just fine."

"I told you." Melvin adjusted his leather work gloves. "I imagine your rush to town is to see Sophie."

Joe's eyes narrowed, wondering what was to come. "It is."

"Good. Don't let your mom scare her away. I like her. She's good for you. You look happier."

"I am happier."

"Your mom will come around. She's just afraid. She hasn't had an easy life. She never got over your dad, and I respect that but sometimes I feel guilty that I didn't encourage her to get out and date and find someone else to love. You boys are all she has. You're her world. She worries, and maybe obsesses, but when she sees you're happy, she'll be happy."

Joe nodded, chest tight, a lump thickening in his throat. His grandfather was right. Despite her own heartbreak, she always tried to make everything perfect for those around her. That was why he didn't want his mom to know that Sophie had answered an ad, and that he was embarking on a marriage of convenience. She wouldn't approve, which was why he fully intended to let her believe he'd found love. It was what she wanted for him, and so what if he found it on the internet? The fact was, he wanted a family, and Mom would adore having grandchildren.

Back in the house, Joe headed upstairs to shower and dress.

As he finished polishing his boots, he glanced up at the

framed buckles on the wall, buckles won during his time on the rodeo circuit. He paused to take in the dozens of glittering silver and gold buckles. He'd been a good bronc rider, and he could stick a bull for eight seconds, but he'd been a great team roper.

He and his brother Sam had been an almost unbeatable team, winning big money together. He'd enjoyed traveling with his brothers on the circuit, too, but when Granddad said he needed one of them home to take on the responsibilities of the ranch, Joe had to be the one to give up traveling and competing. He was the oldest. It was his job to step up and take on the mantle of ranch foreman. He'd grown up on the ranch so it wasn't as if he was a stranger to it, either. But it had been good to get away from Paradise Valley for a couple of years and just live on the road. Free. Unencumbered. He loved his grandfather and Mom but they were both so serious, so weighted by grief that it was hard to breathe sometimes... hard to remember he wasn't an old man. The open road, the rodeo circuit, the company of cowboys, had been such a relief. But he'd been home now for almost six years. Fulfilling his role as the oldest son, assuming the mantle of the Wyatt heir.

He had an odd relationship with the ranch, not exactly love and hate, but sometimes it came close. Because the ranch was an anchor. He was tied to the land, tied to the acreage and boundaries and seasons. He'd never lived anywhere else. He'd grow old and die here.

That was the heaviest part of the anchor, the part that weighed him down.

He would have given up the ranch for Charity if he could have. He'd loved her so much he would have turned the world inside out for her, and if it had only been him, he would have done it. But to turn his world inside out meant he'd turn his mother and granddad's world inside out, too, and how could he do that to them?

How could he choose to be so selfish?

His grandfather had taken them all in, and taken care of them for the past twenty some years, paying all the bills, providing stability, security and leadership. Granddad was strong and determined. He was not going to let his son's widow and boys suffer, and overnight he'd become a surrogate father, attending all their school events with their mom, and teaching them the things their dad would have taught them. Granddad loved them fiercely, so fiercely that Joe couldn't disappoint him by walking away from his legacy at the ranch. It would break Granddad's heart. And so Joe let Charity go, even though it hollowed out his heart.

Fortunately, Charity had moved on, finding love with Quinn Douglas, another rancher's son who'd become a Major League Baseball player, and was living her best life in Seattle.

Joe folded the cloth into the shoeshine box and put the kit back into his closet before putting on his boots. And Joe was going to have his best life, too. Sophie was waiting and from this moment on, there would be no looking back, no regrets. By noon today he'd be a married man.

❧

SOPHIE'S HEART RACED. Her hands weren't steady as she finished applying her mascara. It was her wedding day, at last.

She wasn't wearing a bridal gown, though. Instead, she'd brought a fitted ivory blazer with a pair of wide-legged ivory silk trousers from California for the wedding. The trousers were long and she needed high heels to keep the hem from dragging on the ground, but even in her four-inch bone heels, Joe would still be a full head taller.

She was downstairs, waiting for him, when he arrived. "You look beautiful," he said, as he entered the formal living room at Bramble House.

Her cheeks warmed. He always sounded so sincere when he gave a compliment. "You look nice, too."

And he did. He was wearing a dark jacket over a white collared shirt, with dark denims and dressy cowboy boots. The fit of his jacket made his broad shoulders ever wider and his hips even narrower.

The man had a body, she'd give him that.

"Ready?" he asked.

She nodded. "I have all the paperwork in my purse."

"You don't want a coat?"

"It's nice out. I think I'll be okay."

SHE WAS MORE than okay. Sophie looked gorgeous—sexy—in the slinky ivory suit. She wasn't wearing a blouse that he could see beneath the fitted blazer and the plunging neckline revealed so much smooth skin he doubted she was even wearing a bra. It wasn't a normal daytime look for Marietta and yet she looked smoking hot. He admired her confidence, too. She had style, and she always turned heads.

She'd certainly turned his.

"I should have brought you flowers," he said, feeling a stab of regret. "Shouldn't you have flowers?"

"It's a courthouse wedding."

"Yes, but don't brides need a bouquet?"

"You don't have a boutonniere."

"I don't really like wearing flowers."

Her lips twitched. "Now there's a shocker."

Her mouth was wide and full and as sexy as the rest of her. He wanted to kiss her; he wanted to feel her mouth and body against his, if only to reassure himself that this would work out, that everything would be okay.

Instead, he walked her to the truck and held the door for her before climbing behind the steering wheel and starting the engine.

As he drove the short distance to the courthouse, he refused to think about anything other than keeping to the speed limit, because he didn't know how to marry this way. Didn't know how to get hitched without his brothers here.

Didn't know how to do this without his mom or granddad, either. Everyone would have plenty to say once they learned what happened today.

It hadn't ever been his dream to marry this way. He and Charity—

Joe stopped himself there. No looking back. No comparisons. No regrets. There was only today, and today, Sophie Correia, in her sleek cream suit with her long dark hair and bright shining eyes was going to be his wife.

He should have brought her flowers. If she was going to marry at the courthouse, she should at least have something fragrant and pretty to hold.

SOPHIE'S PULSE RACED as she watched the clerk process their paperwork.

Sophie, who had been the one to press for the wedding, felt increasingly emotional, but she couldn't cry here in the Crawford County Courthouse, and certainly not *now*. This was what she wanted. Commitment. Marriage. The new life in a new family.

And yet, for the first time since leaving Central California, she missed her family. It seemed wrong to marry without any of them here, and yet none of them would support what she was doing. Her dad especially would be horrified. Maybe it was a good thing he wasn't alive anymore. It had always been her dream to have him walk her down the aisle. She had been such a daddy's girl. He'd spoiled her and Sarah rotten.

Sophie reached up and surreptitiously wiped beneath her lashes, drying the moisture with trembling fingertips. No, Dad would not like her marrying a stranger, but he also would not have liked what Leo had done. Her dad had liked Leo. *A lot.* He used to say Leo was another son to him. Maybe it was just as well that Dad wasn't here.

Sophie's chest tightened and she blinked, drying her eyes. There was no reason to cry. Today was a happy day. Today was the first day of the rest of her life.

The clerk glanced up and smiled. "I think that's all the paperwork," she said. "Judge Whitford is waiting for you. Just go up to the second floor, his office suite is on the right side of the elevator."

They climbed the stairs rather than take the elevator and Joe gave her a brief nod before they entered the office suite. She nodded back. They were doing this. She wanted this, even if she was emotional.

The ceremony itself took no time at all, the vows quickly said, then declaring them married even more quickly spoken. More signatures were required afterward, with the judge's secretary promising to return the documents to the clerk downstairs. "We'll mail you the official copy in the next few days."

"Sounds good," Joe answered.

"Do you two have fun plans for the rest of the day?" the

secretary asked hopefully.

"We haven't discussed it," Joe said gruffly.

"What about your honeymoon? Surely you've discussed that."

Sophie darted a glance at Joe. His expression was shuttered and she sensed he was growing uncomfortable and so she stepped in. "It's a surprise," Sophie said brightly. "We're going to go after Easter. Cheaper flights when spring break is over."

"Oh, that's sensible." The secretary sat back down. "Hope it's a good one. A beautiful bride deserves a little romance."

Sophie smiled and followed Joe out of the office and into the hall. He was silent as they descended the staircase to the lobby, but chivalrous as he opened the front door for her. She shot him a side glance as they stepped into the bright spring sunshine. Joe was so quiet. He was almost always quiet, but his silence felt different now. The silence stretched as they walked down the brick steps. Her heart thumped. Her high heels clicked against the brick. The breeze swirled pink petals across the sidewalk. She was careful not to step on them.

She was married.

And numb.

Maybe it was shock, because she didn't feel anything. She didn't feel grateful, or scared, or even relieved.

And then he reached for her hand and held it firmly. "I

didn't even think about a honeymoon," he said lowly. "I'm sorry."

She gave his hand a squeeze. "I never once imagined we'd have a honeymoon."

He stopped in front of his truck and faced her. "You deserve more than you're getting."

"I'm getting you," she answered, facing him, her gaze sweeping his hard, handsome features, seeing the shadows in his clear blue eyes. "Please don't worry. I'm good. I'm happy. I hope you're happy."

"I just keep thinking that a quickie wedding isn't fair to you. Leo ruined your December wedding and now—"

"Now I'm your wife." She stood up on tiptoe and kissed him lightly. "And I wouldn't be here now if I'd married him, so we should be glad Leo dumped me. Otherwise you would have married some other desperate woman and she might not be as wonderful as me."

For a moment Joe's expression was blank and then he laughed, bringing Sophie close. He wrapped his arms around her and hugged her. "You're right; I got lucky."

"Sooo lucky," she teased.

He kissed her forehead and then stepped back. "Should we go celebrate somewhere? Go to the Graff and order champagne with our lunch?"

"Don't you have work waiting? Especially with your grandfather hurt?"

"Granddad is fine. And it's our wedding day. We have to

do something to celebrate, don't you think?"

"I do."

The Graff's formal dining room had just a few guests seated when they arrived, and they were given their pick of tables. Sophie wanted to sit near one of the arched windows with a view of the garden gazebo. Joe ordered a bottle of Dom Perignon when the waiter approached their table.

With their champagne flutes filled, Joe lifted a glass. "To my new wife, Sophie Wyatt."

She blushed and clinked rims with his flute. "May we have many, many happy years," she added.

They toasted again and drank again. And after they ordered their meal, Sophie sat back in her chair. "We did it," she said, smiling, before biting into her bottom lip to keep it from quivering. She felt keyed up, overly excited, and she knew it was nerves, but also something else. Maybe hope? A hint of happiness?

"Yes, we did."

She twirled her delicate glass on the tablecloth. "What do you think?"

"I think it's a little crazy," he admitted.

"I do, too. But maybe it's good to be a little crazy. At least we're proactive; we're going after life, not waiting for it to find us."

"By all accounts, my parents were a little crazy. Mom met Dad while he was competing on the rodeo circuit, and they fell for each other right away. They were practically kids when they married, Dad was just twenty-three, and Mom was nineteen. Rumor has it they married quickly in Vegas when they realized she was pregnant. I don't think her parents would have thrown her out. My mom's parents weren't religious, or particularly strict, but Wyatts don't walk away from their responsibilities, and if Mom was pregnant, Dad was going to do right by her—and their baby."

"Which was you," Sophie said.

"Which was me," he agreed.

She lifted her flute. "Let's toast your parents. To your mom and your dad. I hope your dad, if he's looking down from heaven, is happy."

"To Mom and Dad," he repeated.

They spent an hour eating and visiting, ending their meal with a three-layer chocolate cake, which they shared, before returning to Joe's truck. "I wish I could stay with you all day," he said. "But Granddad—"

"I understand."

He nodded, and opened the passenger door for her. "We probably should talk about the next steps, though."

Sophie waited until he'd settled behind the steering wheel to ask, "You mean, telling everyone? Moving me to the ranch?"

"Yes."

She hesitated. "Do we have to do that right away? Can we just enjoy a little bit of time as newlyweds before the world has to know?"

"You're worried about my mom."

"I've made a commitment to you. We're going to make this work. But maybe we take it slowly for everyone else."

He started the truck and backed out of the hotel parking lot. "How slowly?"

"I don't know. I guess that's what we have to figure out."

At Bramble House he walked her to the front door. "I hate leaving you."

"I'll be fine."

"You look beautiful."

Her cheeks felt hot. She ducked her head, suddenly shy. "Thank you."

"I'll come back for dinner."

"Or just coffee. Make it easy on yourself."

JOE RETURNED THAT evening, taking her to Grey's Saloon where a live band was performing. It was fairly crowded but they found two available stools at one end of the bar and ate dinner sitting at the bar, listening to music.

Joe looked particularly handsome in his blue denim shirt and crisp dark blue Wranglers, the fabric of his shirt taut over his muscular biceps. Sophie glanced at his profile. He was so incredibly good-looking. He was truly a catch. And yet he'd stopped putting himself out there. He'd just given up on dating.

He turned his head and caught her studying him, and he

lifted a brow. "Regrets already, Mrs. Wyatt?"

"No, Mr. Wyatt, just thinking you're a pretty hot cow-boy, and a very hard-working cowboy. There was no reason for you to place an ad for a wife. Ladies probably love you."

"You've seen where the ranch is—it's not all that accessi-ble. The terrain is rugged. I'm often gone all day, maybe even all night, and it's not convenient to head into town to meet a girl for drinks." He caught her expression and shook his head. "You're different. By the time you arrived in Marietta, we'd already gone through the preliminary stuff, and we'd cut to the chase. We knew what we wanted. Which is why the ad served its purpose. It weeded out the women that wouldn't be happy on the ranch. It weeded out women who couldn't handle a long winter without access to town."

"Is it really that bad in winter?"

"It can be, yes. And this past winter was particularly hard. We had three weeks where we couldn't go anywhere, we were completely snowed in, and it was all we could do to take care of our livestock."

"I'd think most Montana women would know that, and would be prepared for harsh winters," Sophie said.

"There's a big difference between winter in Marietta, and winter on our ranch. My former girlfriend—"

"The one your mom liked so much?"

He nodded. "She couldn't handle the remoteness of the ranch. It's essentially why we didn't work. We loved each other, but she needed town, and her sisters, more than she needed me, so…" His broad shoulders shifted. "I don't blame her, either. I respect her for being honest. Far better we end things when we did, than try to make it work, only for it to end in divorce."

"You scare me a little bit with your description of winters. It's called Paradise Valley, Joe."

"Yeah, well it's not really much like paradise six months of the year." Then he leaned forward and kissed her, the kind of kiss that made the hair rise on her nape and her body prickle with awareness. "I can't wait to have you at the ranch," he said, lifting his head, "but I agree with you. I think we should give it a week or two. See how things go and reevaluate."

"Sounds good," she said. Sophie took a sip of her beer and then set the bottle down. "But if I'm going to be in town for another couple of weeks, I need something to do. I can't just sit around all day and wait for my ninety minutes with you at night, Joe—even though they're my favorite ninety minutes of the day." She gave a pat to his arm, and then allowed her hand to linger, savoring the hard carved shape of his bicep and tricep. "This afternoon, I went online and looked at jobs in the area and there are plenty of businesses looking for help."

He shifted on his barstool, not happy. "You don't need to work. You're my wife now. I can take care of your bills."

"Joe, that's not happening. I've been financially independent since I graduated from college nine years ago. I take care of my own bills."

"You weren't supposed to be paying for a hotel room, either, and yet here you are—"

"I don't mind. I'm not complaining. I'm just saying I think it'd be good for me to have a job, and have a purpose. It'll help time pass more quickly, and I'll feel better about myself."

He looked away, jaw hard. "I like it when you're at the ranch. You make it feel… different."

"Different how?" she asked, curious.

"Brighter, lighter, better." He looked at her, managed a crooked smile. "I probably sound needy and emotional."

She laughed out loud. "No, you don't. Saying you enjoy my company isn't pathetic, either. It's a nice thing, and makes me feel wanted."

"You're wanted," he said gruffly. "I look forward to having you back."

"And I will be, once your mom isn't so resistant to having me there."

"This is so not easy. Managing my mom isn't easy—" He broke off, shook his head. "I don't want to be disloyal, but she wasn't well when I was younger and I got mad at her for being sick. I was pretty hard on her for a number of years and it wasn't fair. She was doing the best she could, but I pushed her away and it's only in the last five years, since I've come home, that we've grown closer."

"I understand."

He looked at her, blue eyes cool and clear. "Just know I'm aware this is hard, and I'm aware it's extra hard for you."

"So, what do you suggest, Joe? I'm not being sarcastic. I'm completely sincere. I'll do whatever you think is best. If you think I should move in, I'll do it. If you think we should wait, I'll stay in town. All I know is that I don't want my mother-in-law hating me, so let me look for a job, and we'll just keep seeing each other in the evening and on weekends."

"What kind of job will you look for?"

"Ideally, something in my field. Import-export."

"Montana's top exports are cigarettes, coal, copper, silicon, nothing remotely like your business in California."

"Exports are exports."

"But these export fields are dominated by men."

"I'm familiar with the old boys' club. It's part of every business."

"You won't be welcomed with open arms."

"Huh. That seems to be a pattern around here." She glanced away, battling her temper. Joe didn't seem to realize that he wasn't helping. He wasn't being supportive in any way. "Would you rather I just get my nails done and take an exercise class every day?"

"Is that what you'd like to do?"

"*No.* I like working. I'm really good at what I do."

"Then why did you give it up to move here?"

"Because I thought I could help with your business. I thought I could contribute to your family business. I come from a family business, and spent the past five years working for a family business so I thought I'd be needed, and wanted—"

"You are wanted," he interrupted gruffly.

"But not needed," she added in a low voice.

"Not yet, no, but that will change. I promise."

She studied his expression, but he looked serious, earnest. "I'll look for a temporary position then. I'm capable of doing just about anything in an office, but would be happy to just be busy."

"Would you want a car? Mom's is just sitting there. She doesn't drive anymore."

Sophie arched a brow. "And you think she'd go for that?"

"She might. We'd discussed selling it last November. Leave it to me."

JOE CALLED HER late the next morning to check in. He'd had a sleepless night and he woke up wishing Sophie was there with him. He thought of her all the time, and even when he didn't want to think of her, he could see her face, and the shape of her lips, and the long glossy length of her hair spilling over her shoulder.

He wanted to wake up and see her at breakfast, smiling at him over her cup of coffee. He wanted to walk with her, and take her out on the ranch and show her his favorite places. He just wanted her at the house, settled, so that they could move forward as a married couple.

Same house, same room, same bed.

His body ached and his chest tightened as it struck him that he missed his wife.

"I've begun looking for a car for you," he said. "I wanted some ideas if Mom's car isn't an option."

"I don't think you should talk to your mom about her car. It's her car, Joe."

"She doesn't drive it."

"But she won't want to sell it to me."

"We'll see."

"Do we have a price range?" she asked, still sounding troubled.

"Ten to twenty thousand," he answered, "and don't worry. Everything will work out. I promise."

"Okay." She hesitated. "I have news."

"Good news?"

"I think so."

He smiled. "Then tell me."

"I've got a job! Thirty hours a week to start. Additional hours possible if it's a good fit."

"Doing what? Where?"

"Front desk and light bookkeeping. It's for a hair salon, just a short walk from Bramble House on the way to Main Street. Yesterday, I saw a sign in the window that they were looking for someone to manage their front desk and so I stopped in today and after interviewing with the owner, she offered the job."

"Do you remember the name of the salon?"

"Um… no. Darn it. I can look it up, but it's in a pink house on the corner, if that helps."

Joe closed his eyes. That was all he needed to know. There was only one pink house, or one pink hair salon, in all of Crawford County, and that pink house was the Wright Salon, and belonged to Charity's younger sister, Amanda. At one point he'd spent a lot of time with Amanda because Charity and her sister were inseparable.

"Do you know it?" Sophie said, sounding uncertain.

"I do."

"You're not happy I'm going to be working there? It's not my normal industry but I thought it'd be a good way to meet people in Marietta—"

"That's great. I'm happy for you."

"The owner, Amanda, is really nice, and she needs me. I think they've been without a receptionist for over a week. It was bedlam when I arrived, and I get the job by just jumping in, answering the phone, and helping look up appointments."

"Good for you."

"I can also get my hair done for free. Every month I get to have a free service, whether it's my hair or a spa service."

Joe frowned, picturing her long glossy dark hair. He loved her hair. "What would you do to your hair? It's perfect."

"It's really long. I was thinking I should get a cut that's a little more stylish—"

"Don't," he interrupted. "At least, don't cut it, not anytime soon. You've made so many changes recently, I don't want you to do something impulsive and then regret it."

"You mean, like move to Montana? Agree to marry a stranger?"

He grimaced. "Yeah something like that."

"Well, I'm having fun so far, and I think it's a smart move to have me in town. I'm having fun exploring Marietta."

"Well, we'll have to get you back up here so you can pick up the car. Or maybe Granddad can follow me down, and then take me back up."

"Or, I can take you back up and drop you off. Maybe after we have a date night."

"Speaking of, should I stay over there one night? Our two-hour dates aren't that satisfying."

She didn't answer for a long time. "You could," she said, hesitantly.

"You're not ready," he said bluntly.

"Not quite yet," she answered apologetically. "But soon, though."

"Understood." But he was disappointed. He seemed to need—and want—her far more than she needed and wanted him. But at the same time, he'd been single for years. She'd only recently come out of a serious relationship.

"I'm going to train at the salon this afternoon," she said, filling the awkward silence, "and then if you don't mind, I was hoping to work tonight. The salon stays open later on Thursday nights. But if you don't want me to—"

"No, do that. That's smart to just jump in. Do you know your hours yet?"

"Tuesday through Saturday right now, ten to six. The salon is closed Sundays and Mondays, although Amanda will come in for certain clients. I guess she does a lot of weddings."

"Hope you have a good day. Call me when you're off tonight. I'll look forward to hearing all about it."

"You have a good day, too. Say hi to your mom and grandfather for me."

"Will do."

FOR SOPHIE, THE day passed so quickly. She couldn't even believe she'd been at the salon seven hours by the time she helped Amanda close up the shop. It had been a fun day, too, fast-paced and filled with really nice people.

Amanda had shown her how to work the computer and use the salon software to check clients in, and book appointments, and look up individual stylist rates. Sophie took dozens of notes, typing them into her phone, so she'd have a cheat sheet to help her remember passwords, and how to do things, including how to close at night.

"You're a fast learner, Sophie," Amanda said to her as they turned out the lights together, and set the security alarm before stepping out the front door. "I'm impressed."

The wind was cold and grabbing at their coats. Sophie bundled her arms over her chest, trying not to shiver. "I really enjoyed today. It's fun to work with so many young women. My last job was mostly men, and mostly older men. This is a breath of fresh air."

"Well, you're a breath of fresh air. You have such a great attitude," Amanda said, locking the dead bolt and slipping the keys into her pocket. "What brought you to Marietta?"

Sophie felt a little uncomfortable. She wasn't sure how to explain it to others, much less her boss of seven hours. "I met someone online and it got serious and so here I am."

"You moved here for a guy?"

"Yes."

"He must be pretty special."

Sophie grinned. "I think so."

Amanda's winged brows arched higher. "So it's serious?"

"Yes."

"How serious?"

Sophie hated not being totally truthful, but how could she tell the truth? She and Joe had agreed to keep their secret until the time was right to share with others. "We're getting married… soon."

Amanda's eyes widened. "How long have you known each other?"

"A couple months."

"And you're really getting married?"

"It's the plan."

"But you just met him." Amanda's brow creased. "Why get married so soon? There's no need to rush—" She broke off, expression concerned. "You don't *need* to get married? You're not pregnant are you?"

"No. Not pregnant. Haven't even had sex." Sophie blushed. "We're taking the… physical… stuff slow."

"He's either a saint, or he's not into women," Amanda said as they headed to the curb.

Sophie's cheeks felt so hot they had to be bright pink. "We just want to make sure we're in this for the right reasons."

"So, who is this amazing guy?"

"I don't know if you'd known him. He's not really social."

"What does he do?"

"He's a rancher. His property overlooks Pray in Paradise Valley."

Amanda froze on the sidewalk. "Are you talking about one of the Wyatts?"

"Yes. Joe." Sophie's heart did a painful little jump. "Do you know him?"

Amanda hesitated, a strange expression on her face. "Very well. He used to date my sister, Charity. They were together a long time."

Sophie blinked, caught off guard. "Did she read romances?"

"Why?"

"Joe said his last girlfriend got along really well with his mom. They'd pass books back and forth and watch *American Idol*—"

"That's Charity."

Sophie felt like she'd swallowed broken glass. Her stomach hurt. Her heart hurt. "Mrs. Wyatt really liked her."

"Joe and Charity were together a long time. My sister loved him. He was her first love, and it took her a long time to get over him. Fortunately, she's found her right person and is happily married, but there was a period there we weren't sure she would be able to move on."

Sophie was still trying to take it all in. "Why did they break up?"

"I think the ranch was a big issue for her. She struggled with the idea of being so far away from town and me. We've always been really close and she couldn't imagine not being able to see me often, because in winter, you can't get into town all the time, not from their property."

"It's only a thirty-minute drive."

"In good weather. Bad weather… blizzards…" Amanda's voice trailed off, and she was silent a moment before adding, "But Joe adored her. He treated her like a queen. He would have done anything for her… anything but give up the ranch. It's his legacy."

"The ranch has been in his family a long time," Sophie said.

"Seventy, eighty years. Something like that."

"Joe took it hard when they broke up?"

"Very hard, but Charity struggled, too. For years, Charity compared every guy she dated to Joe, and none were good enough. But then she met Quinn and she could finally get over Joe Wyatt."

Sophie pictured her Joe—tall, broad shouldered, handsome, with those cool blue eyes—and she wondered if he'd smiled more when he was younger. Had he smiled more when he'd been with Charity? Or had he always been serious? "What's Charity like?" Sophie asked, suddenly feeling insecure.

"She's lovely. Sweet, kind. She's the nurturer in the family."

Sophie didn't think anyone would ever describe her as sweet, kind, or a nurturer. If anything, she'd been told to not be too ambitious, not too assertive. She'd been told more than once to tone it down, hold back, don't come on quite so strong. *Men don't want to feel like they're in competition with a woman. It's okay to lean on them. It's okay to make him feel like the man*, Mom would say.

Sophie pressed her lips together, holding back the wave of emotion. Leo had left her for her sister, Sarah, a preschool teacher, who was, well… soft, sweet, nurturing.

Men apparently liked nurturers.

Sophie's chest ached with her bottled air. She forced herself to exhale. "So, you have nothing bad to say about Joe?"

"Oh, my gosh, no. I'm glad Joe's found love. I'm glad he's found you. He's a really good guy. Lots of the girls around here had a crush on him, but after things ended with Charity he turned his back on Marietta. Glad that he's found his happy ever after."

CHAPTER SIX

WHILE SOPHIE SPENT Thursday night working at the Wright Salon, Joe was having dinner with his family. During the meal, his grandfather seemed more chatty than usual, but his mother seemed tense, and Joe wondered if she was hurting. She didn't like to be asked, though. Inquiries into her health made her feel like an invalid, but the fact that she'd phoned her doctor to request an appointment indicated her pain threshold was being tested.

Tonight might not be the best night to mention that he was car shopping, but if not tonight, then when? His grandfather would never get younger. His mother would never be cured. This was just life, and he needed to navigate it to the best of his ability.

After clearing the plates and making and pouring coffee for his mom and himself, Joe returned to the table, placing his mom's coffee in front of her before he sat back down with his cup.

"I'm looking for a car for Sophie," he said without preamble. "She didn't bring hers out, and her family is selling it for her in California. She'll need one here. I've found a couple good possibilities." He sipped his coffee and then looked up, his expression deliberately bland. "I'm going to check out a couple different cars Saturday afternoon if either of you want to go with me?"

Granddad's ears perked up. "What specifically are you looking for?"

"A small SUV, preferably with four-wheel drive," Joe answered.

"Is that what she drove in California?" his mom asked.

"No, but California city roads and Montana mountain roads are two different things."

"So she's staying in Montana then," Granddad said.

Joe checked his smile. Granddad sounded almost approving there. "I think so. She has a job. She's working at Amanda's hair salon as a receptionist."

His mom's jaw dropped. "She's working for Amanda?"

Joe nodded. "It's temporary, until she finds something in her industry but she was excited about it. She likes to keep busy."

Melvin's gaze met Joe's. "Your mom's car is just sitting there," he said.

Looking at his grandfather, Joe had to check a smile. They were so much alike. They had the same blue eyes, the same build, the same tough exterior. Joe sometimes wondered if his dad had been the same. He didn't remember him. He just remembered the afters—after the accident, after the move to the ranch, after his mom changed so much. "I'm not touching Mom's car. That's her car, her present. I'll find something used and affordable for Sophie."

"But you never know the history of a used car," his mom said, speaking up. "Used cars can be very unreliable."

"But affordable," Joe answered.

"It needs to be able to handle the roads come winter. Ice, snow, potholes. No road." His mom frowned. "If she's still going to be here that long."

"She'll be here," Joe said confidently.

"You think so?" His mom sniffed. "California girls are delicate—"

"You're a California girl," Joe interrupted with a wink. "And look at you now, twenty-six years in Montana and still going strong."

His mom drummed her fingers on the dining table. "How much are you thinking of spending?"

"Ten to fifteen thousand. Twenty if the car's immaculate and has low mileage."

"Joe, that's a lot of money."

"I know, but I want to keep her safe."

She stared at him long and hard. "How much did you spend on my car?"

"Mom, it was a birthday present. I'm not divulging numbers."

"It was expensive, though, wasn't it?"

"You only turn fifty once, Mom."

"Joe, stop being a smart aleck—"

He laughed quietly and shook his head. "You haven't said that since I was a kid."

"Then don't be irritating. Tell me what you spent."

He leaned back in his chair. "A lot more than what I'm going to spend on Sophie. You're my mom, and she's my"—he took a breath—"girlfriend, and I just need something to give her some freedom and mobility."

"I hate for you to spend fifteen thousand, or more, when my car is sitting there in the garage, rusting away."

"It's not rusting. I take care of it for you. And I'm not giving your car to Sophie."

He gave her a look, his expression intent, but hopefully, loving. "You don't like her, Mom, and she wouldn't ever accept it, knowing it's yours, knowing it'll probably upset you."

Summer slapped the table with both hands. "Now you're just talking nonsense. I do not dislike Sophie. I have never said one unkind word to her—"

"Maybe not, but you've never said one kind word," he interrupted, leaning forward to take her hand in his. "Mom, she's not the enemy. She's not stealing me away. I'm not going anywhere."

"You're spending an awful lot of time in Marietta, though."

"Because she's there. But hopefully she can come up here, too. The weather's getting warmer. It'll be summer soon. It'll stay light late."

"I'll sell my car to you," Summer said, pulling her hand out from under his and rising. "Eleven thousand five hundred and you can invest that money into some stocks for me. I have a list of stocks I'd like you to buy." And then she walked out.

Joe sat there with his grandfather for a moment, before Granddad looked at him, a faint smile in his light eyes. "That's the outcome you wanted, wasn't it?" he asked.

"It's a good deal. Blue book value is twice that," Joe answered.

"Well, there you go," Granddad said, getting up from his chair. "Things are working out."

AMANDA HAD NO idea she'd given Sophie serious food for thought, but as Sophie walked back to Bramble House after leaving the salon, she replayed the conversation she'd had with Amanda about Joe and Charity, curious, but also baffled. It boggled her mind that Charity, who apparently loved Joe so much, wouldn't move to the ranch for him. That didn't make sense to Sophie. It wasn't as if the drive was hours long. There was no traffic between the ranch and town. How could that distance be too much? *If you loved someone, didn't you try?*

Once back in her room, Sophie kicked off her boots and stretched out on her bed to call Joe.

"How did it go?" he asked.

"Good. There's a lot to learn but Amanda was super patient and really sweet. She's got to be the nicest boss in the world."

"Glad it went okay," he said.

Sophie paused, giving him an opportunity to say he knew Amanda, or to say that he liked her, having once been rather close to her. But he said nothing and she suddenly didn't feel like she could bring Charity up over the phone.

"How's your grandfather's face? Is he all bruised up?"

"He's healing, which means, yes, he's quite blue and yellow."

"Dinner went well?"

"Roast chicken and boiled potatoes."

"And you made that?" she asked.

"I did."

"You're pretty talented."

"I just don't like being hungry," he answered.

"Will I see you tomorrow?" she asked.

"I'm hoping to take you to dinner and a movie tomorrow night. Would that work with your schedule?"

She winced, feeling guilty. "You're my number-one priority," she said. "Whatever you want works with my schedule."

"Then have a look at what's playing at the theater in Marietta and see if anything appeals to you. I can pick you up from work tomorrow at six and we could go straight to dinner."

"I like it. See you then."

JOE SPENT THE afternoon the next day washing, waxing, and detailing his mom's dark green Jeep Wrangler so that when he showed up in Marietta, he'd have a pristine car to give to Sophie. The Jeep had less than eleven thousand miles on it, and hadn't been driven in the past eighteen months except for brief outings to keep the battery from dying. It had been a new car Joe had bought his mom for her fiftieth birthday three years ago, but her arthritis made driving too painful and after the first six months, the Jeep pretty much sat in the garage.

Joe was glad she'd decided to sell it to him. There was no way he would have ever been comfortable just taking it from her. By buying it, he ensured there would be no guilt trips later.

He made sure he was waiting outside the pink hair salon before six. It was sprinkling a little, but he was wearing his cowboy hat and the brim kept the rain off his face. He wished it wasn't raining, though, not after all the time he'd spent waxing the Jeep. But even in the drizzle, it was shiny, and looked virtually brand new.

Sophie came outside a few minutes after six. She looked puzzled as she approached him. "Where's your truck?"

"At home."

"Is it not running?"

"It's fine. I just wanted to drive your new car to you." He reached into his pocket and pulled out the car key and car fob. "It's actually not a new car. It's three years old but it has very few miles and only one driver." He hit unlock on the Jeep and the lights flashed. "What do you think?" he asked, handing her the key ring.

She looked at the Jeep and then him, and then back to the Jeep. "This is an expensive car, Joe."

"I got a very good deal on it."

"But still—"

"Sophie, don't always worry about money. I'm not hurting for cash." He walked to the driver's side, opened the door for her. "Tan interior, leather seats, the seats are heated, too, which you'll appreciate come fall. Four-wheel drive so you could go off-roading if you want."

She made a face as she slid behind the steering wheel, "Do I look like an off-roading kind of girl?"

"I don't know. But you sure look pretty in that car."

Sophie flexed her hands against the steering wheel, and glanced around, admiring the interior. "Joe, it's beautiful. I don't know what to say."

"As long as you're happy."

She reached up and tugged on his coat, drawing him down. She kissed him. "Thank you. You spoil me. I'm not used to it, but I appreciate it."

He kissed her back. "You are more than welcome. Now, are you good to drive? We're just heading to the Chinese restaurant next to the theater. I think we have enough time for a quick bite before the seven fifteen show."

THE NEXT WEEK passed quickly, with them falling into a routine they both enjoyed. They'd work and then meet for dinner or, in some cases, an after-dinner drink. They were enjoying a dessert date at Main Street Diner Thursday night when Joe mentioned she'd been in Montana two weeks today, and it was there at the diner they'd had their first date.

Sophie wrinkled her nose as she licked the buttercream frosting from the prongs of her fork. "I wouldn't call that a date. It didn't feel like a date. I was so nervous. You made me so nervous."

"Me? You were crying even before you met me," he retorted. "You got off the plane in tears."

"I know. Two flights, one big layover. It gave me way too much time to think."

"What were you thinking about?"

"That life sure can change in just a few months."

Joe's smile faded. "Do you still miss him?"

"Who?"

"Your ex."

"Oh, Leo." Sophie shook her head. "No. Not at all."

"Why not? You were together a long time."

She wondered if he was comparing her and Leo to his relationship with Charity, but Charity didn't leave him for another man. Charity didn't cheat on him by starting to see his brother...

"I met him because I worked for his family business," she

said after reflecting for a moment on what she could say without revealing the whole sordid Sophie-Leo-Sarah debacle. "Brazer Farms is one of the biggest dried fruit exporters in California, based in Central California, an hour or so from where I grew up. I interviewed with them out of college, started as an assistant to the export manager, and gradually worked my way up. Leo headed up sales, and we spent a lot of time together at work, and then began to spend a lot of time together outside of work. We weren't a stay-at-home couple, though. We were always going somewhere, always busy, and because of our careers, we had a lot of business events and parties to attend. Looking back, I think we were too busy pretending we were a good couple instead of being a real couple."

Joe's brow lowered, his expression one of disbelief. "That doesn't make sense to me. You weren't a real couple?"

"A lot of energy went into what people saw—flowers to me at the office, dinners at fancy restaurants, vacations at posh places." She glanced down at her plate, feeling a little heartsick at the memories. It didn't feel good remembering Leo or the past. She still didn't know all the details about his relationship with her sister, only that there was a point where they both developed feelings for the other, and somehow they forgot to tell her.

Her eyes suddenly prickled and her chest ached with suppressed emotion. She really didn't want to sit here and talk about Leo. She didn't want to think about the past. This was why she was in Montana. She had a new life now. She had a new family, new friends, new work. Just thinking of new friends and work, she thought of Amanda. Sophie really liked Amanda. Amanda was stylish and smart and funny— and incredibly compassionate.

"Amanda told me her little apartment above the salon will be available next week," Sophie said, changing the subject. "The person renting has moved to Missoula and Amanda said she can cut me a really good deal so that it'd be a lot cheaper than Bramble House. What do you think?"

Joe didn't look very excited by her suggestion. "You're enjoying Marietta?"

"It's a really cute town. I do like it."

"You want to stay in town?"

"Well, I have to stay somewhere."

"How do you feel about moving up to the ranch?" he asked. When Sophie didn't immediately reply, he added, "I want you there."

Sophie hesitated. "Your mom?"

"Truthfully? Her arthritis is really bad right now. Her hands are so swollen she can hardly grip anything with her left hand. She's booked an appointment to see her doctor but she can't get in for another week."

"Your poor mom. Why didn't you tell me?"

"I'm telling you now."

"How long has this been going on?"

"I don't know. It's hard to say. She gets quiet when she

hurts. She doesn't talk a lot about her pain, but I noticed she was moving slower, and sleeping less. Once I became aware of her discomfort, I talked to her, and realized she's struggling." Joe hesitated. "I've liked coming to town and seeing you. I really enjoy our time in Marietta. It's been good for me, getting off the ranch, but in the end, I can't escape the ranch. There's no running away from it."

"You don't have to run away from it. It's your home."

"But it's not been a comfortable place for you, and I hate to ask you to move up there—" He broke off, brow furrowing. "I worry about you there, but I worry about my mom when I'm here. I don't know how to juggle both."

"You shouldn't have to. That's not fair to you." She pushed her plate away. "You know, you don't have to come see me every night. I look forward to seeing you each night, it's my favorite part of the day, but if it'd be better for us to just see each other on weekends—"

"No."

"If your mom is in pain, is she going to want me there?"

"It's my home, too, Sophie, and I try to be respectful of my mom, but I need you up at the ranch. I need to see your face more. You have the best smile and it kind of does it for me."

Sophie blushed and grinned. "I had no idea."

"I think you had a little idea." Joe kissed the tip of her nose. "Anyway, I've discussed this with Granddad. He agrees with me that you should move in."

"He does?"

Joe nodded. "It would mean you'd be doing a lot of driving every day, but the car is relatively new and should be reliable."

"I love the car."

"Will you mind an hour driving every day?"

"Not at all," she said. "And I want to do whatever I can to make this easier for you and for your mom."

He exhaled and gave her a faint smile. "I knew you'd say that."

"We knew this had to happen sooner or later."

"It'll be a change," he said. "It won't be easy. You'll get put to work. I'm afraid you'll soon miss the freedom you had here in Marietta."

"I didn't come to Montana for a vacation. I'm happy to take on cooking, and grocery shopping. Happy to do the laundry and cleaning. I've worked hard my whole life. I'm not a princess. I don't expect anyone to wait on me."

"There's a lot of work at the ranch. It can feel endless."

She leaned forward and reached for his hand. His hand was big, calloused, warm. He laced his fingers with hers, and she immediately felt safer, happier. "When you advertised for a wife, you made it clear you were looking for someone to help lighten your load. You made it clear that you needed a partner, not just for the good times, but also for the hard times. Please don't try to protect me. I don't need that. What I need, is to support you now. I need to help your mom. My

135

mom's grandmother was in a wheelchair the last twenty years of her life. She lived with us for most of that time. It wasn't easy, but life isn't easy."

His fingers tightened around hers. "Let's move you in, then. I think I'll start sleeping better once you're under the same roof."

"I don't work Saturday. I could pack up my car and head up in the morning."

"Or, I move you up tomorrow night, and you'd have all day Saturday to settle in."

She pictured moving up to the ranch after a long day on her feet and it didn't sound appealing at all. "Can we wait until Saturday? I'd rather feel rested and refreshed before I descend on her."

"If you think that's best."

"I do." But Sophie's stomach churned and her nerves returned. She wasn't as confident as she used to be. She'd never doubted her worth before, but she struggled with insecurity now. "Are you going to tell her that I'm coming? I think you should give her some warning. I have a feeling she'll take the news hard. I'm sure she's still not comfortable with the engagement... can you imagine how she'd react if she knew we were already married?"

"That's a bridge we don't have to cross yet. We will tell her we're married when we're ready to tell her. And frankly, maybe by being around you more, she'll accept that we are committed, and going to stay together. Perhaps this is good this is happening. Mom just needs to see how your presence at the ranch makes things better, not just for me, but for everyone."

"I can only hope," Sophie answered.

He studied her face, his expression gentling. "It's going to be fine."

"Yes," she agreed, but her voice wasn't quite steady.

He lifted their linked hands, and kissed the back of hers. "It might not be okay right away, but it will eventually be okay. My mom is not a monster. She's afraid, and worried that I will be hurt. She's also probably worried that she's being replaced, and worried about all the things she can't control, but she doesn't have to protect me. You're not Charity, and I'm not Leo, and we're not going to walk away from each other."

SATURDAY MORNING, AFTER waking at five, Joe made coffee and headed to the barn to look after the horses. Granddad was in the kitchen when Joe returned. "Looking forward to seeing her here, aren't you?" his grandfather asked.

Joe grabbed the skillet to fry up sausage and eggs. "I worry about Mom, though."

"She'll be fine," Melvin answered, drawing out a chair at the old kitchen table. The scuffed pine table had dominated the kitchen for nearly seventy-five years. It had been one of the first pieces of furniture built for the house by Joe's great-grandfather, Melvin's father. "You'll be fine, too. Don't worry so much."

"I don't—" Joe protested.

"You do," Melvin answered. "That's because you're the firstborn. You can't help it."

"You don't worry?"

"Wasn't the firstborn."

Granddad had an older brother who died in Vietnam. He never talked about him, but every now and then a reminder came up and Joe knew that even if his grandfather didn't talk about the people he'd loved who had passed, it didn't mean he'd forgotten them.

"Want eggs?" Joe asked.

"No. I'm meeting Fred Carlisle for breakfast in Livingston. I hear he's considering selling his place in Clyde Park. Big spread. Lot of land."

"Isn't a lot of that acreage higher up?"

"The property goes from low to high. It's got a couple rivers and a lake. Good for fishing and hunting. He's thinking someone might want to buy it and turn it into a dude ranch." Melvin's tone revealed his distaste. "But I suppose people have to make a buck somehow." He rose from the table. "Want me to drop you off in town on my way? Might put your mind at ease if you're in the car the first time your girl drives up here."

"It would."

"Can we leave at seven?"

"I'll be ready."

❧

SOPHIE WAS HAVING breakfast in the Bramble House dining room when Joe walked in. Heads pivoted to watch him as he crossed the room to her. He looked rugged and almost unbearably handsome in his boots and hat.

"Morning," he greeted her.

"Good morning." She rose and kissed him hello. "This is a surprise."

"You have all those suitcases and two flights of stairs," he said. "Figured you could use a hand."

"Well, let's get out of here then," she said. "I've packed up everything but it's still in my room."

With Joe's help, they were able to make just one trip down with her luggage, and while Joe loaded everything into her car, she went to check out. Eliza Bramble told her the room had already been paid for, and gave her a hug, and told her to stay in touch.

Outside, Sophie found Joe leaning against her Jeep. "You paid for my room," she said.

"I did."

"I can pay my own bills."

"And I can pay your bills, too."

"I don't want to be an extra expense."

"Sophie, are we going to do this our whole marriage? When do you let me start taking care of you?"

Her mouth opened, closed. She didn't have an answer for that because she wasn't accustomed to anyone paying for things for her, or taking care of her. She'd been pretty much on her own for years now. "Are you going to let me contribute to ranch expenses?"

"No."

"Why not? I'll be living there."

"Because the ranch pays for itself."

"Then what's my income for?"

"It's for you to decide."

"So you don't care what I spend my money on?"

"No."

"So I could spend it on you?"

He gave her a look like she was impossible. "If that's what you want to do. Now let's get on the road. You're driving. I want to see how well you can do on our rough roads."

"I can handle your rough roads. Just watch."

"I will. Let's go home."

HOME. SUCH A strange word, Sophie thought, as she drove south on Highway 89. The one-lane highway wasn't quite familiar yet, but she loved how pretty it was this morning, everything green along the sparkling, splashing blue of the Yellowstone River.

As she drove, Joe told her a little bit about the town of

Pray, and how it had a population of roughly six hundred and fifty people. Twenty-five miles south of Marietta, and thirty miles north of the entrance to Yellowstone, the town consisted of about five acres, and was privately owned, with the current owner both the mayor and sheriff.

She was trying to soak up everything she could since Paradise Valley was going to be her forever home.

That was a strange thought, too.

She'd spent her life in California. She'd only traveled a little bit, mostly to Lake Tahoe for skiing and San Diego for beach vacations, and those trips had usually been organized by Leo since he liked nice hotels with nice pools.

"Have you done a lot of traveling?" she asked Joe.

"When I competed, yes."

"Where did you go?"

He shrugged. "Pretty much everywhere in the US, except for Hawaii, and Alaska."

"Every state has a rodeo?"

"Surprisingly, yes."

"Wow." She glanced at him with fresh appreciation. "Is there any place you haven't been that you'd like to go?"

"Australia," he said promptly. "I'd like to go there. One of my friends married a girl from New South Wales and I'd like to visit them."

"You should."

"*We* will," he said, emphasizing the we. "Just as soon as I can get someone to cover the ranch for me."

141

"One day, maybe."

"Hopefully sooner than that. Thinking it could be a good honeymoon."

"That'd be amazing."

"I think so, too."

CHAPTER SEVEN

THE DOGS BARKED as they arrived, but their tails were also wagging. Sophie noticed that Runt's huge tail was wagging awfully hard. Maybe he wasn't quite so scary after all.

Joe directed her where to park, in the open spot near his big black truck. The dogs circled as they unpacked her Jeep, sniffing her a bit, but then ran off when they heard one of the ranch hands opening a far gate.

Inside the house, there was no need for another tour. Sophie remembered the basics, and when Joe carried her luggage up the stairs to the second floor, they both hesitated in the narrow hall, uncertain as to the right bedroom for her.

Mrs. Wyatt emerged from her bedroom at the end of the hall, and sorted their indecision out for them, saying that Sam's room would do nicely for Sophie, and Joe, of course, would have his room.

"I'm not comfortable with you sharing a bedroom here," Summer said. "I know you're both adults, and independent, but since you're not married, you need to be sensitive to your grandfather's values."

Sophie's face burned. "I understand completely," she said, ducking her head, feeling embarrassed and yet also relieved since she wasn't ready to share a room, or a bed, with her new husband. She didn't know when she would be, and so if she could overlook Mrs. Wyatt's stern tone, and judgmental expression, Sophie was happy with their sleeping arrangements.

"I'm sorry I'm old-fashioned," Mrs. Wyatt added, without sounding the least bit apologetic. "Now, if you had your own house, that would be different, but this is your grandfather's house and it would be disrespectful to shack up under his roof."

"I'll just unpack," Sophie said, slipping away, and closing the door.

Joe watched the door to Sam—not Sophie's room— close, and waited until he heard the click before he faced his mom. "That was a little heavy-handed, Mom. You're determined to make Sophie as uncomfortable as possible."

"That's not true. I just think it's important we be upfront about expectations and rules."

"But shack up? Come on, Mom, I don't think anyone says that anymore."

"Sorry I'm not hip and cool."

He rubbed his face and counted to ten. He didn't understand his mother. She had never been so unreasonable before. She'd adored Charity, had welcomed Charity with open arms. Why couldn't she be a little more welcoming for

Sophie? "You don't have to be hip and cool. I just want you to give Sophie a chance. You'd like Sophie if you spent any time with her. She's really a nice person, a very kind person, and while she doesn't look anything like Charity, she's actually a lot like her."

"Well, I guess I'm going to get that opportunity now that she's staying here." Summer paused. "Just how long is she staying here for?"

"Forever." He saw his mom's eyes widen and he battled his temper. "We're engaged, and we're going to marry soon."

"How soon?"

"Very soon," he repeated. "A week? Two weeks?"

"Is she pregnant?"

"*No.*"

"You can tell me the truth."

"Mom, trust me. Sophie is not pregnant."

His mom shifted the cane, resting her weight on it. "You don't have to rush into anything. You've only just met—"

"Don't do this. Don't come between us. I'm marrying Sophie. She's going to be your daughter-in-law, the mom to my kids, and we want kids. We're excited to start a family. I'm hoping by Christmas we'll have one on the way."

"I just don't understand why everything is rush, rush. Get married soon, then, but take some time to be a couple in love. Enjoy the freedom—"

"Let's not kid ourselves, Mom. I don't have a lot of freedom. I'm not complaining, but I'm pretty much tied down here, and have been tied down here, for years. Getting engaged to Sophie is the first thing I've done for myself since returning home five plus years ago. I should be allowed to make some decisions for myself."

Summer held his gaze a long moment before sighing softly. "So I guess we're planning a wedding."

"We'll handle that, Mom."

"No, if you're going to get married, we need to do it properly. Can't have people thinking it's a shotgun wedding."

"I don't really care what people think."

"I don't care what people think, but I also won't have them talking about you. It's not fair to your grandfather, either. He deserves to see his oldest grandson married well."

Joe had to hand it to his mom. She wasn't just stubborn. She was relentless. "What does that even mean?"

"A minister, a church, a nice reception with a sit-down dinner—"

"That's not what Sophie and I want. We want small, intimate, *private*."

"Your granddad doesn't go to church every Sunday, but he reads his Bible and prays twice a day. He'll want to see you married by a minister."

"Sophie and I were thinking Las Vegas, just like you and Dad did."

"It broke your granddad's heart that JC and I married in Vegas. Don't do it. We made a mistake. Have your wedding here so he can celebrate with you. We'll also want to invite the neighbors, and your brothers, of course. Sophie's family, too. Does she have a big family? How many do you think we'd be inviting?"

"I can't answer that."

"Either way, we've got a lot of planning to do, and all that planning takes time—"

"We're getting married in two weeks—"

"Impossible to plan a wedding in two weeks! You can't even get invitations printed in two weeks."

"Then email everyone."

"We're doing this right. We need a month at least, Joe—"

"Too long. That's too stressful."

"Three weeks, then."

Joe shot a desperate look at the closed door to Sam's room, glad Sophie couldn't hear this, but also dreading the moment he'd break the news to her that there just might be a wedding in the works. "Fine. Three weeks, but not a day longer."

SOPHIE COULD HAVE sworn she heard Joe and his mother discussing a wedding in the hall. She tried to listen through the closed door, but the walls were thick, and the door was solid, and she only caught every fifth word, which seemed to be wedding, wedding, wedding, wedding.

Dear God, his mom wasn't trying to convince Joe that

he needed to marry her?

She closed her eyes and drew a slow breath, trying to ease the panic building. It had seemed so easy answering the ad, and flying to Montana, but since arriving, it had been anything but easy.

Things went from challenging to complicated to impossibly complicated.

Maybe they just needed to tell Mrs. Wyatt the truth. They were married. End of story.

And yet she pictured Mrs. Wyatt's face, her blue eyes the same cool blue as Joe's, and Sophie pictured her eyes turning glacier blue.

Sophie really didn't want to be frozen out.

She needed Mrs. Wyatt to like her. It would be intolerable living in this house together if they were enemies.

Later that evening, she crept from her room and knocked softly on Joe's bedroom door. He opened almost right away, wearing sweatpants and a faded red T-shirt. She'd never seen him in sweats or a T-shirt, and he looked amazing. His upper half all hard muscular planes and thick biceps, while the dark heather-gray sweatpants hung from his lean hips, revealing a flat, chiseled abdomen.

She must have spent considerable time admiring his physique because when she finally looked up into his face, one brow was lifted quizzically, and his lips were curved. "Do I meet your approval?"

"I've just never seen you in anything but those really stiff

Wranglers and button-down shirts," she said, blushing. "You're quite... fit."

"Thank you. I think?"

She rolled her eyes and stepped past him to enter his room. "You look good and you know it." Sophie quietly closed the door behind her before turning to face him. "I heard you and your mom talking in the hall earlier tonight. I couldn't hear everything but I could have sworn she mentioned a wedding, and you... agreed?"

"As you know, she had some concerns about you being here, but I told her it's not temporary, that we don't want a long engagement, and that we're planning on being married soon."

Sophie sat down on the edge of his bed. "That's not really what I heard, though."

His arms folded across his chest, drawing the faded red T-shirt higher, revealing more of his impressive abs. "What did you hear?"

She tore her attention from his body to his face. "I thought you agreed to a wedding, in a month's time."

"I'm sorry, I did."

"Oh, Joe."

"I know." He rubbed the back of his neck. "I'm sorry. I don't know how to handle her lately. She's impossible, and difficult. I don't want to lose my temper, and so I give in to keep from getting angry. But maybe I should just get angry—"

"No. Don't do that."

"I'm at a loss, Sophie."

"I know, me too, but we'll figure this out." She sighed, remembering the bits and pieces of the conversation she'd overheard. "It's as if she wants us to have a real wedding with a real reception." Sophie had visions of the long-sleeved white satin bridal gown that had once hung in her closet, and the lush red and cream and green floral bouquets that the bridal party would have carried. She'd dreamed of a Christmas wedding since she was a little girl. She loved Christmas and nothing seemed more romantic. Leo had obliged, proposing one Christmas, and agreeing to marry in December of the following year. "We didn't want one of those, remember?"

Joe walked the length of his bedroom floor and ended up at the window overlooking the valley. The moon was just a sliver in the sky and all was dark beyond the glass. "I know." He turned to face Sophie. "They didn't, either, because they went to Vegas. Maybe that's why this is so important to her. Maybe it's why it's so important to Granddad. My mom seems to think he'd be hurt if he wasn't present at our wedding, and if it's important to him, it's important to me. My granddad—"

"Is everything to you, I know." Sophie drew a slow breath. "So this is for him?"

Joe nodded. "And my mom. I think it's important to her, too."

"But we can still make it small and private, right? We're not doing a formal reception. We're not inviting lots of people. It's you, me, and your immediate family, right?"

"Right."

"Okay," she sighed, defeated. "We'll get married again, so they can be there, but I'm not buying a wedding gown, I'm not going to wear a veil—"

"You can't wear that suit, though. You'll need to get a new dress."

"Joe!"

"I'm sorry. My grandfather's old-fashioned. That sexy ivory suit would give him a heart attack."

Sophie squeezed her eyes shut, thinking this proposed wedding was already a mistake. "Fine, I'll look for a simple, sweet, affordable dress." She opened her eyes, fixed her gaze on him. "But it's not going to be white, and not bridal, but something I can wear again."

"Fine."

SUNDAY MORNING AFTER breakfast, Joe told Sophie to dress warmly. He was going to take her out on the property in his truck. "I thought you'd like to see some of the ranch."

"I'd love that." She ran upstairs to change, passing Joe's mom in the hall. "Good morning, Mrs. Wyatt. How did you sleep?"

"I slept," Joe's mom answered. "How about you? Was it

difficult in a strange bed? I never used to sleep well in other people's beds."

"I actually slept quite well. I loved the quilts on the bed. It was toasty warm."

"The nights get cold up here."

"It was chilly this morning when I woke up." Sophie gestured to her outfit. When she'd gotten out of bed she'd pulled a sweater over her flannel pajamas and she'd put on fuzzy socks. "I might need to get some fleece-lined slippers."

"You could find some at the Mercantile in Marietta."

"I'll check on Tuesday." Sophie smiled and slipped into her room, thinking that hadn't been such a bad conversation. In fact, Mrs. Wyatt had been almost maternal. Maybe things would improve now that Sophie was here.

Sophie loved the day spent with Joe out on the ranch. She got to see the cattle—or at least one big herd—as well as a lot of the Wyatt land. They headed off the road at one point, bouncing across a pasture so Joe could straighten a leaning fence post. Sophie sat in the truck watching him work, his body lean and powerful. She found it incredibly sexy watching him work. He was so comfortable in his body, so self-assured.

He'd brought apples, ham, cheese, and some day-old biscuits with them and they had a picnic sitting on his truck's tailgate. They were high in the mountains, and the sun was shining brightly in the blue sky. A few clouds floated overhead. The view was amazing. The valley stretched below, the dark navy of the Yellowstone River just a glimmer against the green poplar trees. A hawk circled above them. Sophie tipped her head back to watch it, even as she listened to the breeze rustling the pine tree branches. "It's so peaceful. You're in God's country up here."

"Yes." He turned his head and looked at her, his expression intent as he studied her. "Think you could be happy here?"

"Yes."

"Your family is a long way away."

"I can always get on a plane and go home if I feel the need."

"Would you come back?"

She heard something in his voice, something unsure, and it was the first time she'd ever heard him sound unsure about anything. She put her hand on his denim-clad knee, and left it there. "I will always come back to you." She patted his hard knee. "We're a team now, you and me."

"You are impossibly beautiful," he said, his deep voice pitched even lower. "And strong and kind."

"I wish I felt that way."

Joe's eyes met hers for a moment, and she saw heat in his blue eyes, heat and something she couldn't define. Then he kissed her.

Sophie had been kissed, and she'd been kissed, but this... this wasn't any kiss she'd ever known before. He gathered her against him, holding her firmly to him as his mouth took hers, claiming hers. The kiss was hot, fierce and intense. She could feel Joe's hunger, feel his need. She'd known he was attracted to her, and she'd seen the desire in his eyes before, but as he pushed her back in his truck and stretched out over her, his mouth and body were telling her in no uncertain terms that she was his.

It was both heady and seductive, and her pulse drummed hot and fast, her body melting beneath his.

One day soon they'd consummate their marriage. One day soon she'd belong to him completely.

His hand slid through her long hair, before caressing her face. He knew just how to kiss her, knew just how to get her to sigh and want.

She wanted, and yet she still had so much fear… so much anxiety.

When would Joe realize he'd made a mistake?

When would he get tired of her?

And what would life be like on this ranch when he no longer needed her physically?

Suddenly her eyes were smarting and she felt a tear slip free. Joe felt it, too. He pulled back and gazed down at her. "What's wrong?"

"Just so many emotions," she said, trying to smile despite the telltale tear. "Ignore me."

"I'm not going to ignore you," he said, wiping away the tear. "Why are you sad?"

"I worry you'll get tired of me—"

"Never."

"You can't say that. You hardly know me."

"How can I get tired of you? You're mine."

She reached up to touch his hard jaw with that tantalizing rasp of beard. He hadn't shaved this morning and she liked it. "I got that from the kiss. You, Tarzan. Me, Jane."

He looked surprised for a moment and then he reluctantly smiled. "That obvious?"

"I'm not complaining. That was probably the hottest, sexiest kiss of my life."

He smoothed her long hair back from her face. "We're just getting started. I wouldn't even call that an appetizer."

Her lips curved. "You make me smile."

"Good. That's the way it should be."

And then he kissed her, gently, before drawing her up. "We should head back. Don't want anyone wondering what happened to us."

ON TUESDAY JOE stopped by the Wright Salon, bringing her lunch. "What are you doing?" she asked, darting a glance into the salon where Amanda was working. Joe and Amanda had yet to meet face-to-face since Sophie had started at the hair salon.

"Mom's in the car. She has her doctor's appointment today but I thought you might like lunch. It's chicken salad. If you don't want the bread, there's a fork in there so you can pick the chicken part out."

Sophie stepped around the front desk and gave him a kiss on the cheek. "That is so nice of you. I wish you could stay and have lunch with me but I know you're in a hurry. Hopefully, the doctor will have something she can try to help with her pain."

He kissed her goodbye, the brush of his lips sending a delicious shiver up and down her spine. Then he was gone, walking out the door of the salon. Sophie's heart skipped a beat as she watched him walk.

Her new husband was ridiculously sexy.

"He's matured nicely," Amanda drawled from the doorway.

Sophie blushed and looked at Amanda, unable to hide her smile. "He's pretty cute, isn't he?"

"The Wyatt brothers all inherited the handsome gene. Every one of them is good-looking. Charity used to say that she and Joe would make the prettiest babies in Crawford County—" Amanda caught herself, and broke off. "Sorry. That wasn't appropriate."

"It's fine. You have your own history with Joe and the rest of the Wyatts."

"Seeing as I put my foot into it, let me just add that you and Joe will make really pretty babies, too. Pretty and feisty. Neither you nor Joe are a pushover. I have a feeling your kids will be born with a spine of steel."

Sophie returned to the ranch late afternoon and did a

load of laundry before returning to the kitchen to start dinner. Joe usually met her there once he was done with his work.

In the kitchen, in the middle of the long pine breakfast table was a stack of bridal magazines.

Sophie nudged the stack. There were three different magazines, the latest edition of *Modern Bride*, *Montana Bride*, and *Western Weddings*. Sophie quickly restacked them and then seasoned the roast before putting it in the oven, but the entire time she prepared the meat, she was terribly aware of the magazines.

When Joe joined her to make the mashed potatoes, Sophie pointed to the magazines. "Where did those come from?"

"Mom bought them when we were in town today."

"Why?"

"I think you know why."

"I don't need bridal magazines," Sophie said lowly, standing at the sink, side by side with Joe while they both peeled the potatoes.

"They're not for you, they're for her," he answered.

"Why does she want magazines?"

"To see what the trends are now. She's curious." He reached for the final potato, able to peel two for her every one. "I'm sure your mom looked at magazines when you were planning your wedding."

Sophie opened her mouth, then closed it. There was no

point arguing with him, because yes, her mom had looked at magazines, and gone to a wedding trade show, and sat there while Sophie interviewed a wedding planner.

"There's nothing to stress about," he said, chopped up the potatoes on a cutting board, knife slamming against the board. "She's just happy for us."

Sophie didn't have to look at the set of his jaw to know he was working to contain his temper. She could hear it in every hard chop of his knife. Joe wasn't happy, but she didn't know if he wasn't happy with her, or with his mom's interference. Either way, Sophie wasn't going to say anything, at least, not tonight. Tempers were already running high.

It only took one night at the Wyatt's to discover the family's habit was to listen to the national news after dinner. Joe would record it, and then they'd all gather in the family room to watch the news together after dishes were done.

Tonight, as Sophie took her seat on the couch in the family room, she spotted a printed checklist of wedding to-dos next to Mrs. Wyatt's armchair.

Sophie eyed the checklist nervously, as that particular list came from a popular wedding website. She'd used that detailed list to help her plan her wedding to Leo. Just seeing the distinctive font and layout with all the little boxes to be marked made her nauseous.

Sophie struggled to concentrate on the news, but found herself sneaking glances at Mrs. Wyatt who was casually leafing through *Montana Bride*.

The checklist.

The bridal magazines.

The folder with pictures on Mrs. Wyatt's lap.

By the time the news wrapped up, Sophie was in agony. What was Mrs. Wyatt doing? What kind of wedding was she imagining?

Another half hour passed, and suddenly Sophie couldn't stand the suspense any longer. "What are you looking at?" she asked Joe's mother, her voice not quite steady.

"Photographs from a wedding north of Livingston, in Clyde Park. They had the reception in a barn," Mrs. Wyatt said, turning the magazine around and flashing the full-page spread at Sophie.

Sophie saw green and gold and a smiling bride being swirled around by a handsome cowboy groom.

"Do you know them?" Sophie asked.

"Oh no, just getting ideas," Mrs. Wyatt answered, briefly glancing at Sophie over the top of the glossy magazine before resuming her reading. "I think a barn wedding could be really charming."

Sophie's hands knotted in her lap. She told herself to be calm. Everything would be fine—if she cleared the air, and adjusted expectations. "Ideas for what?" she asked carefully.

"Why, your wedding."

Sophie darted a glance at Joe but he appeared lost in his columns and calculations. She sensed he was deliberately lost, choosing to be obtuse so that she had to handle this instead of him. "Joe and I are thinking we're just going to get married by a justice of the peace in Marietta. We already have the blood test results, and all our paperwork."

Mrs. Wyatt turned another page, her gaze seemingly riveted to whatever was on it. "You don't want a minister?"

"I don't think it's necessary. Neither of us attend a church here—"

"But you don't have to attend a particular congregation here. A number of the local clergy will perform the ceremony, whether at their church, or at another location." Mrs. Wyatt tapped her iPad and opened a fresh window. "The Methodist and Lutheran ministers both would. I know, because I spoke with them yesterday. The trickiest part would be finding a date that works in their calendar. Obviously, the further out, the more available." She smiled brightly. "Joe, could you scoot down on the couch so we can talk without having to shout?"

She waited for Joe to shift closer to Sophie. "We need to make some decisions tonight," she said. "I'm concerned we won't be able to get everything done if we don't start making decisions. I'm happy to call and book things, but I need to know what our approximate head count is going to be. Getting the head count is important because it influences everything we do, from the number of invitations we order, to the venue, to the size of the cake." Summer glanced from Sophie to Joe and back to Sophie. "I have a list of people I want to include, and it's approximately seventy-five people—"

"Seventy-five people?" Joe interrupted. "Mom, we have a family of six, with no cousins or aunts and uncles to speak of. Where are you getting seventy-five guests from?"

"Our rancher neighbors. The MacCreadies, Carrigans, Sheenans, Vaughns, Hollises, Douglases, Tates... oh dear, who am I forgetting?"

"About six more families. But, Mom, you can't invite every ranching neighbor."

"Why not? They're always looking out for us, and it's time we included them in something. We spend too much time only worrying about ourselves."

"That's because we're a little bit removed overlooking Pray."

"Even better. And don't you want them to meet Sophie? That way they know who she is and can keep an eye out for her."

"Put that way, yes, fine."

Mrs. Wyatt looked at Sophie. "Now you come from a large family so we could easily be inviting twenty-five to thirty people, right?"

Sophie shook her head. "No. I'm not inviting my family. It's a long way to come. It'd be at least two flights for most, and that gets expensive."

"No one? Not even your mother and father?"

"My father passed away a couple years ago and my mom doesn't travel on her own."

"What about brothers or sisters? Couldn't one of them

bring your mother?"

"Not on short notice."

"What about friends?" Mrs. Wyatt persisted.

Sophie felt Joe's hand slip into hers and give a faint squeeze. She gave a squeeze back, grateful for the gesture of support. "I think it would be difficult for people to come from California on such short notice, and I'm good with that. I really would prefer a small, simple ceremony without any fuss."

Mrs. Wyatt looked baffled. "Surely, there is at least one person you'd like to invite?"

Sophie thought of her family, and then her colleagues from Brazer Farms. Her family and her work were so intertwined, there was no way to separate one from the other, not anymore. "Maybe I could invite some of the girls from the salon in Marietta. Amanda had already offered to do my hair, so maybe she and her husband could be included?"

"Charity's sister?"

"Sophie works for Charity's sister, yes," Joe said. "I think that's a great idea to have Amanda and her husband come."

Mrs. Wyatt looked at them for a long moment before slowly, laboriously typing notes on her iPad. She then turned to her son. "Joe, what about you? I've already put your brothers on the list, but wasn't sure which of your friends you'd want to invite."

"I don't really have anyone to invite, either," he answered. "I've lost touch with most of the guys I went to school with. I'd probably just invite Sam, Billy, and Tommy. They're my best friends."

"I can't believe there's no one else," she said.

"Lots of the neighbors you're inviting are my friends. If I happen to think of anyone else, I promise to tell you."

Mrs. Wyatt looked down at her iPad and scrutinized her list. "So ninety people roughly? Twenty-five to thirty invites?"

Sophie gripped Joe's hand hard. He just gave her a faint shrug.

"Mrs. Wyatt," Sophie said as calmly as she could, "that's a lot of people. Maybe too many people?"

"That's just who we're inviting," Mrs. Wyatt answered. "Who knows how many will actually come?"

THE REST OF the week passed and Sophie was ambivalent about the weekend. She was looking forward to being off work Sunday and Monday, but she had a feeling Mrs. Wyatt would be keeping her plenty busy discussing this proposed wedding.

She cornered Joe in the kitchen Saturday morning where he was reheating a cup of coffee. "Joe, you have to help me. We didn't want a big reception. We were happy with how we got married. I think we're just going to have to tell your mom we're already married."

"Have you seen my mom's expression? Have you seen

how happy she is? She's on cloud nine. Who knew that planning a wedding was all she's ever wanted to do?"

"But we don't *need* a wedding. We don't need a party. We don't need all this fuss." She wrapped her arms around his waist, and tipped her head back to look into his face. "Please tell me we aren't really going to do this."

Joe's arms circled her, his hands low on her back. "Would it be such an awful thing to have a second ceremony? Would it be the end of the world to have this reception?"

"*Joe.*"

He shrugged. "I don't get the whole wedding hoopla myself, but she's having so much fun."

"Then you come sit with her and look at the magazines. You study flowers, and discuss cake, and debate beef or chicken for the dinner entrée. I can't do it. I told you when I arrived that I never want to plan another big wedding—"

"And you're not having to plan it. My mom is happy to organize everything."

"That's not the point."

"What is the point? Because I'm confused."

"We were going to do a quiet, practical ceremony—"

"Which we did."

"And there was not going to be any fuss."

"And there was no fuss."

"But now, suddenly, we're keeping our marriage secret *and* agreeing to a wedding that makes us the focus of everyone's attention and, Joe, it's overwhelming. I'm not good with attention. I don't want to have to playact our way through the entire reception, but we will."

"We'll just stay on the dance floor the whole time so no one can talk to us."

She made a face. "And I'm a terrible dancer."

"I'll help you."

Sophie closed her eyes. "This will not end well," she said darkly.

"Let's be optimistic."

"Okay, fine. I'm *positive* it's going to blow up in our face."

He laughed softly and pulled her into his arms and kissed her. "At least you make me laugh."

His kiss was so good, so persuasive that Sophie promptly forgot what they were talking about, and stood up on tiptoe to feel even more of him.

They were still kissing when Granddad walked in and they quickly broke apart.

Melvin Wyatt looked from one to the other and then shook his head. "No need to look so guilty. I'm not the kiss police."

Sophie and Joe looked at him, and then each other, before bursting into laughter.

"I like him," Sophie said, when Mr. Wyatt had exited the kitchen.

"I do, too."

❧

MRS. WYATT LOVED her iPad because she could talk to it, and Siri would help her find the things she wanted without having to type everything into the search engine. She also seemed to be very proficient at looking things up because every day, Joe's mom had new saved searches for Sophie to look at. On Sunday, the list was endless—

Rustic country wedding invites.
Country wedding decor.
Chic barn weddings.
Hay bale couches.
Barn wedding ceremony ideas.
Cowboy wedding cake.
Cowboy wedding ideas.
Cowboy wedding centerpieces.

Sophie chewed the inside of her cheek, trying not to panic as Mrs. Wyatt clicked from search to search, pointing out all the exciting possibilities. The photos were beautiful, but there was a level of planning, and execution, which made Sophie's head spin.

"What do you think?" Mrs. Wyatt asked, looking up from a screen filled with picnic tables covered in white linens, featuring lanterns and bright summer flowers plopped in pale green canning jars. "This would be a really pretty reception idea for a May wedding. Emerson Barn already has tables and chairs. Not sure about the size, though. I think they have rounds in several sizes, and then we'd just have to rent the linens and get the flowers—"

"Flowers are really expensive. It doesn't matter what kind they are."

"We're not poor. We can afford flowers, and good food, and a live band. Besides, I want my boys to have proper weddings. I've dreamed about them growing up, falling in love, starting families of their own. I made a promise to JC that I'd see his boys raised right, and having a real wedding is part of that promise."

When Sophie didn't immediately reply, Mrs. Wyatt added, "Are you good with a barn wedding? The Emerson Barn isn't available on any Saturdays in May, but we could do a Sunday? The last three Sundays are all free right now, although May tenth is Mother's Day and I don't think we should try to schedule a wedding for Memorial Day weekend. So that would leave the seventeenth. I do think that's the best day, don't you?"

"I agree," Sophie murmured weakly.

"I'm happy to make calls tomorrow to reserve everything. I just want to be sure this is what you and Joe want. So the third weekend of May?"

"Maybe I should go get Joe. We want to make sure he approves of the date, too," Sophie said, trying to hide her dismay, before excusing herself to search for Joe.

She found him in the barn fixing a bit on one of the bridles. He lifted his head, a hint of a gleam in his light eyes. "How are the wedding plans going?"

"Your mom is really invested in it, Joe. A little too invested."

"She's been in a very good mood lately."

Sophie leaned on a stall and watched Joe work. "Her ideas aren't cheap. She's turning it into a fancy wedding."

He glanced at her from beneath the brim of his hat. "I thought it was a barn wedding. She mentioned the Emerson Barn to me."

"Barn weddings aren't inexpensive, and certainly not the way she's thinking of it. Her searches are for 'rustic chic' and 'elegant barn weddings.' She's talking a live band, and dozens of fresh flower centerpieces and two kinds of cake." Sophie tried hard to keep her voice calm and neutral. "Joe, we don't need a big three- or four-layer cake."

"Tell her that."

"I'm trying, but she's just so... enthused."

He tugged on the bridle's leather straps, and satisfied, hung it up. "I'm glad the two of you are spending time together. This is what we wanted, wasn't it?"

"Two dozen floral arrangements will cost at least a thousand dollars."

He looked at her, hands on his hips. "I can afford that."

"And even a simple BBQ dinner will still be about forty or fifty dollars a person."

"I can afford that, too."

Sophie sagged against the stall, realization dawning. "You're excited about the wedding."

He grimaced. "I wouldn't use the word *excited*, but I don't mind renewing our vows and then having a big party for our friends and family. It gives me a chance to introduce you to everyone, and you're gorgeous. Why shouldn't I want to show you off?"

"Everyone's going to ask how we met."

"We tell them the truth. We met on the internet."

"Folks here are pretty conservative. Won't that shock some people?"

"Maybe." Joe grinned. "But sometimes it's good to give people something to talk about."

"I've done that, just last December. It wasn't fun, trust me." She hesitated. "Looks like the third Sunday in May is going to be the big day. Are you okay with that?"

"Yeah, fine. Wish we could do the first Sunday, but I understand why that's a little impractical."

"Oh, and one more thing. Who is JC?"

Joe looked at her, expression guarded. "My dad. Why?"

Sophie felt a pang in her chest. "Your mom said she'd made a promise to your dad to raise you right, and seeing her boys married properly is part of that." She swallowed. "So I think that means we're really doing this."

He put his arm around her shoulder and dropped a kiss on her nose. "I could have told you that the day Mom brought the wedding up. If there's something you should know about my mom, it's that she almost always gets her way."

"She's that stubborn?"

"She's that smart."

CHAPTER EIGHT

B Y WEDNESDAY, THIRTY-THREE wedding invitations had been mailed out.

Joe's mom had found an online company that could print the invitations and mail them directly, all within forty-eight hours. The invites were cute and very country, the printed paper resembling a bit of lace over weathered wood, with the words *We're Getting Hitched* at the top, beneath the knot of twine.

And now that the invitations were out, there was no turning back.

Sophie still felt queasy when she thought about a reception, with a country band, a catered dinner, and a tiered wedding cake. It just felt ridiculously extravagant, adding to Sophie's sense of guilt. There was no need for a second Montana wedding. The courthouse wedding was perfectly legal and they already had the finalized document back from the clerk, but Mrs. Wyatt was so excited about their relationship for once, and even Granddad had pulled out his suits and best boots on Thursday, asking Joe if one of his suits would do, or if he needed something more formal.

Joe had decided that the groomsmen would wear brown leather vests over white button-down shirts, cowboy hats, and dark Wrangler denims. Sophie understood why Joe wanted all three of his brothers in the wedding, if they could make it back, but she had no one to form a bridal party as she was fine with that. Instead, she asked Melvin Wyatt if he'd walk her down the aisle, and he gruffly agreed, giving her a hug, and the hug meant the world to her. It had been a long time since she'd felt wanted anywhere, and the ranch was starting to feel like a second home. If only there wasn't so much emphasis on the wedding. Mrs. Wyatt had arranged for Sophie and Joe to do a cake tasting next Monday since Sophie wouldn't be working, and for Joe's sake, she accepted the news with a smile, but she didn't care about cake, and didn't want to discuss the merits of raspberry or lemon filling for a white cake. She also didn't care if the table rounds should be rounds of six or eight. And, no, she and Joe had no preference for the song for their first dance.

The fact that she felt forced into this farce of a second wedding made her short-tempered and increasingly frustrated with Joe. Joe was thirty-three. Why couldn't he say no to his mom? A simple *no* would have stopped things. Five little words—*Hey, Mom, we're already married*—would have nipped this charade in the bud. Instead, Sophie was putting an incredible amount of energy into pretending to be happy, which had the effect of making her unhappy.

Friday morning, she drove into Marietta to work, her

stomach in knots. She parked on the street a block from the pink house with the white picket fence, always careful not to take one of the spaces in front of the salon as the senior customers might need a close spot.

The wind whipped her long hair and tugged at her coat as she walked to the salon, but the fresh air felt good. Bracing. Sophie was glad to be away from the ranch working today. She needed the distraction. She didn't want to think about the wedding, or hear about the RSVPs starting to come in. She just wanted some time with Joe, and maybe it was selfish, but she wanted to feel like a couple, and have fun, and not worry so much about everyone else.

She knew Joe wanted her, but she worried his feelings were different than hers. She was becoming deeply attached to Joe, but what did he feel for her? He desired her, but was that all it was? Physical desire didn't last forever. Would what he felt be enough for the long term?

Falling in love wasn't part of the plan, and Sophie hadn't planned on developing real feelings. Yes, she'd liked his photo and his profile, finding his blunt *Wife Wanted* ad appealing after the heartbreak with Leo, but she hadn't thought she'd fall in love with Joe... at least, not so fast.

She'd thought it might take years for them to come together, years for them to form a bond, and yet here she was, three weeks into her stay in Montana and he was all she thought of, and all she wanted. And that was what was getting her down... she wanted more time with Joe, not less, and when she was with him, she wanted more of them, and less of his family.

Just admitting that made her feel guilty because she'd known when she arrived in Montana that Joe lived on the ranch with his mother and grandfather. She knew the ranch was isolated. She knew Joe would spend long days outside on the property. But she'd thought they'd have the evenings to themselves. She'd thought they'd have more... what? Romance?

Joe, however, seemed oblivious to her tension, happy to bury himself every evening in market prices and calculations while Sophie inwardly stewed, wanting more, and not knowing how to be content without more.

Fortunately, it was a busy morning at the salon and Sophie kept her smile firmly in place as she welcomed customers and answered the phone and booked appointments. She was beginning to recognize the weekly customers, the older women who came in for a shampoo and style, as well as the young women who liked a regular blowout.

Sophie thought she'd done a good job of hiding her pensive mood until Amanda joined her at the little table in the kitchen everyone used during break.

"You seem to smile a little less every day," Amanda said, removing the lid from her salad. "What's wrong?"

"Nothing's wrong," Sophie answered, forcing a smile and sitting taller. "Why?"

"Hmmm, I don't know exactly what it is. But you seem a

little less glowy today. Is the wedding prep getting to you?"

"Maybe, just a bit, although I feel bad even saying that as Mrs. Wyatt is doing most of the work."

"Weddings can become all consuming."

"Exactly." Sophie frowned as she thought about her life since moving into the Wyatt's ranch house. "It seems like all we talk about right now is the wedding."

"Tyler and I fought the most just before our wedding. It'll get easier, I promise."

"I hope so." Sophie nudged her turkey sandwich, no longer hungry. She did feel sad. Sad and teary. "I might be a little homesick, too," she admitted. "The thing is, I don't want to be home, but I'm struggling a little here. Everything is so new and different and I don't want to fight with Joe, but he doesn't really understand how isolated I feel at the ranch. Our relationship is new, and the wedding is getting bigger and bigger, and there's no time for us just to be together. We both work, and then when we're free, we're always with his family. I like his family too, but I need more time with Joe. I need..." Her voice faded, and Sophie reached up to knock away a tear before it fell. "This is silly. There's no reason for me to cry. There's nothing wrong."

"Moving is hard. Starting a new life in a completely different place is hard. My sister, Charity, has found it tough in Seattle, and misses Marietta a lot." Amanda wrinkled her nose. "But I don't suppose you want to hear about Charity."

"I have no problem with your sister."

"You'd like her if you met her. Charity is really sweet, and fun."

"You're close."

"Very close. BFFs."

Sophie picked at her sandwich. She and Sarah had once been really close, too. Her chest burned, and her stomach cramped. She put her sandwich down, as a lump filled her throat. She missed Sarah. She missed her family. But at the same time, she didn't want any of them here. They wouldn't be okay with her marrying Joe, someone who had been a stranger just a month ago. They'd be upset she was 'rushing' into something with him, would try to convince her to return to California.

Her feelings for Joe had become complicated, too. She had feelings for him—very strong feelings—thus the tears and the anger and the increasing frustration. She didn't want a paper relationship. She wanted the real thing. She wanted Joe to have real feelings for her.

"By the way," Amanda added more brightly, "I just got the invite to your wedding. Tyler and I are definitely coming."

"Oh, good," Sophie said, smiling brightly to hide the sheen in her eyes. "I'll know someone."

"Are you really not inviting anyone from your family?"

Sophie shook her head. "It's just so far. Two flights, and then the drive from Bozeman, which means everyone would need a rental car plus hotel." She glanced up and saw the arch of Amanda's eyebrows. "Okay, it's not just the time or expense. I'm uncomfortable inviting my family. They'll all have something to say about Joe's and my relationship and I don't really feel like hearing it."

"Haven't they met him?"

Sophie shook her head. "They don't even know him."

"What?"

"They know I've come to Montana for a fresh start. They think it's a job opportunity." Sophie grimaced as she tore the crust off a slice of bread. "So there is that to explain."

Amanda blinked. "Wait, *what*? Why? What's going on?"

Sophie pushed her lunch away and propped her elbows on the table. For a moment she just felt fear, and anxiety, and then she looked at Amanda and her concerned expression and had to fight fresh tears. "Can I trust you?"

"Of course."

"You won't say anything to anyone?"

"No."

Sophie hesitated then blurted, "I met Joe online."

"Right. And…"

"He'd placed an ad for a wife." Sophie gauged Amanda's reaction and when none was coming, added, "I answered his ad for a wife. And here I am."

"You're kidding."

Sophie pursed her lips and shook her head. "Nope."

"Wow. I had no idea."

"Yeah, no one does, and I guess that's a good thing?" She

smiled weakly and toyed with the plastic around her sandwich. "I'd just come out of a bad breakup and I thought Joe's ad sounded perfect. He sounded perfect. And, actually, he is. I'm falling for him, and yet that's not part of our deal. We're not supposed to fall in love; we're supposed to be practical."

"I can't see Joe marrying someone he wasn't attracted to." Amanda's lips curved. "Trust me, he's not *that* practical."

"Then why did he place the ad?"

"Knowing Joe, he wanted a relationship but he lives thirty minutes outside of town and women don't just wander on to the Wyatts' property. It's not easy to meet someone when you live on a ranch as remote as the Wyatt's."

Sophie thought about this for a moment. "He apparently had a lot of women answer his ad."

"I'm sure he did. The man's hunky, and he's financially solvent, smart, successful, and incredibly loyal to his family. He's marriage material. And now he's yours."

HE'S YOURS.

Amanda's words stayed with Sophie as she drove back to the Wyatts' at the end of the day.

Amanda had no idea how accurate her words were, because Joe was already Sophie's husband, even though it was in name only.

It felt weird having a husband that wasn't totally her husband.

It felt weird marrying someone without getting intimate.

It felt weird getting married to someone she really didn't know.

It felt weird to be living in Montana.

It felt weird not to have her own place anymore.

In short, nothing felt normal or familiar or comfortable. And there was nothing Sophie could do but deal with it, and learn to get comfortable with the uncomfortable.

SOMETHING WAS OFF with Sophie. She'd been unusually quiet at dinner, and had barely eaten anything, using her fork to move food from one section to another.

When the meal ended, she stood and began to gather the plates, but she didn't look at him and made no eye contact with anyone.

Joe frowned, worried. "You're not coming down sick, are you?" he asked her.

She shook her head. "No."

"Nothing's going around at the salon?"

"No." She finally glanced up but her gaze only met his for a split second before shying away. "Why?"

"You just seem… off."

"I feel fine," she said, carrying the plates to the sink and setting them on the counter while she filled the sink with hot water.

"You hardly said a word tonight."

"I just have things on my mind."

"Like what?"

She added a squirt of dish soap to the hot water. "I was thinking I've been in Montana three weeks now." She flashed him a half smile, but the smile didn't reach her eyes. "A lot has changed in three weeks."

He eased the drinking glasses into the hot soapy water. "Is that why you've been in a mood all week?"

"*I've* been in a mood?"

"Yes. Everyone's noticed."

She faced him, hands on her hips. "Just who is everyone?"

"The point is, if you're upset, you should talk to me."

"We'd have to actually spend time together for that to happen."

Joe could feel his temper stirring. "What does that mean?"

"I came here for you. I came to Montana for you. But we're never really alone, not unless we're cooking dinner or doing dishes."

"Because there's the wedding to plan—"

"But I didn't want the wedding. I wanted *you*."

"Is that why you're upset? Because of the wedding? If so, let's just call the whole thing off—"

"Now you say that! But this isn't about the wedding, Joe,

it's about us. There is no us. It's just work, and then the news, and then bed, and then we do the same thing the next day, and the next day."

"That is life on a ranch," Joe said, gathering the silverware from the table and dumping it into the sink, feeling blindsided by the attack. "It's not all fun and games—"

"I don't expect fun and games. But I would like more of a relationship with you!"

"I don't get it. I'm here. All the time."

"But we don't have alone time. We don't do things, just the two of us."

He said nothing and she turned away, and attacked the first of the dishes. "Are you happy with the way things are?" she asked after a long minute as she scrubbed a plate. "Because it doesn't seem like it to me."

He turned away from her, battling to tamp down his frustration. He didn't want to fight. He didn't like conflict. He hadn't married Sophie to have drama, either.

For several minutes, they both worked in silence, Sophie washing, while he transferred leftovers to Tupperware containers. He carried the empty casserole dishes to the sink. "Move over," he said gruffly. "I've got this. You go."

"Go where?" she asked helplessly. "I have nowhere to go. I have no one here in Montana but you."

The crack in her voice made his chest tighten and ache. He'd tried hard to help her settle in, tried hard to let her know she was wanted here, but if she wasn't happy, what else could he do? What more did she need? "I don't know. To your room? To read a magazine, take a bath, maybe go take a walk—"

"You're not stuck with me, you know." She choked, facing him, tears shimmering in her eyes. "It's not a done deal, yet. You can get out of this—"

He closed the distance between them, his voice dropping. "You're giving up like that? You want a divorce already?"

She dropped her voice, too. "I'm just saying no one knows—"

"*I* know."

"And I know, too, but I'm realizing that the only reason you're getting married in the first place is to make your mom happy, and that, my friend, is not the reason to get married!"

"What about you?"

"What do you mean?" she demanded.

"You're marrying me because your heart was broken in December and instead of trying to get out there and meet someone new, you just answer an ad—"

"Yes, *your* ad!"

"But you're not who you pretended to be."

"I'm not?"

He huffed a breath. "You're emotional. You're sensitive. You're full of feelings and you're the last woman who should agree to a practical, businesslike marriage."

"But that is what I want—"

"Stop. Be honest. You want romance. You want flowers—"

"I wouldn't turn down flowers, or another nice dinner date. I'd enjoy a fun cocktail at a swanky restaurant, but I also enjoy just driving around with you in your truck. I loved eating cheese stuffed in a cold biscuit sitting on the back of your tailgate and watching a hawk circle overhead. That was fun. This, fighting with you, isn't fun."

"Do you know what I want?" he retorted. "I'd like to carry you upstairs and strip off your clothes and spend all night learning your body. I want to see you and feel you and do things to you that would make your mother blush. But instead we're planning a wedding neither of us want, just to make other people happy. We're doing dishes because there's no one else here to do them. We're being mature adults even though it's boring and unsatisfying, because sometimes life is just boring and unsatisfying."

"But we don't have to be boring and unsatisfying."

"So what do you want? Right now, what do you want to do?"

"Let's go find a private corner somewhere and be alone."

"If we end up alone, I'm going to take your clothes off, and do things to you. You good with that?"

She wrinkled her nose as if to disagree, but her voice wasn't quite steady. "Why wouldn't I be?"

"Because you, Sophie, want to be married, but I'm just not sure you want to be married to me."

She took a step back. Her lips parted but no sound came out.

"I think you're still hung up on Leo," he added quietly.

She shook her head. "That is so not true!"

"Then why don't you trust me?"

"I do trust you."

"Why don't you talk more about your family and your life in California then? I'm an open book. You're here with us, you see me, you know me, but there is still so much I don't know about you."

"Joe, I've told you almost everything. My family are dairy people. My dad died several years ago. My mom still lives on the dairy farm in her own house. My older brother runs the business now—"

"And Sarah?"

Sophie stilled. "What about Sarah?"

"Why don't you answer her texts? Why don't you ever speak to her? I've seen her messages. She misses you—"

"You don't know anything about it."

"Then tell me!"

"As soon as you tell me about Charity, and why it's been… oh, five years or more since you dated. Did she break your heart that badly?"

A low clearing of the throat from the doorway was enough to silence them both. Sophie froze, uncertain how long Joe's grandfather had been standing there.

Melvin Wyatt looked from one to the other, expression

giving away nothing. "We've been waiting to turn on the news. If you're not interested…"

"I'm interested," Joe said tightly. "We haven't finished the dishes, though."

"Hard to finish when you haven't even started," Melvin answered.

"Give us just a minute, Granddad. We'll get these done in no time," Joe said.

"Leave them alone," Melvin said. "They can wait, as I have a feeling you'll just start bickering again if left in here to your own devices."

Sophie could tell Joe was embarrassed that they'd been caught fighting, and she was embarrassed, too, but when Joe stalked out of the room without another word to her, Sophie wanted to throw something at him.

Instead, she dried her hands, and waited a moment for her pulse to slow, and then she followed, taking her usual seat on the couch, but tonight placing a pillow between her and Joe.

He glanced at her, arched a brow.

She made a face and turned to stare at the TV screen.

Melvin settled in his leather recliner. "Are we good now?"

"We're good," Joe said shortly.

"Just great," Sophie added brightly.

The national news was filled with breaking headlines and concerns about the national and global economy. There were stories about rising oil prices, political races, and frightening viruses. And Sophie listened, but could tell that this evening Joe's mom was watching them rather than the evening news.

As the program wrapped up, Mrs. Wyatt took the remote and muted the TV. "Is this really what you're going to do tonight? Just sit here, again tonight?"

Joe glanced up, brow creasing. "What's wrong, Mom?"

"You two act like an old married couple already. You'll have plenty of time for that later, when you are an old married couple. Why don't you dress up and head into town? Have a proper date night. You haven't had a date since Sophie moved in."

"It's okay," Sophie said. "We're happy here with you."

Mrs. Wyatt focused her attention on Joe. "Sophie's come a long way to see you, Joe. She doesn't want to just be cooped up at the house. Go to Marietta, go to Livingston. Have dinner. See a movie. Take her dancing. Have fun."

"I've things I need to do here, Mom, and Sophie's happy just relaxing at the house. She's worked all week in town—"

"Sophie, what do you normally do on a Friday night in California?" Summer interrupted, turning to focus on Sophie now.

Sophie saw Joe's jaw tighten. "It depends, but I would probably get together with my girlfriends and we'd go get dinner, or meet for drinks."

"You'd get out of the house."

Sophie hesitated a fraction of a second. "Yes."

Joe sighed, clearly annoyed. "But she's not home with her friends, Mom. She's here with me, and you, and she's enjoying being here. She knows I don't run around a lot. She wasn't expecting nonstop entertainment."

"What about any entertainment?" Summer retorted. "You're not making any effort. You're acting like she's already married. But Sophie is a beautiful young woman, and young women like to be spoiled and fussed over, especially when they've traveled thousands of miles to see their man." She gave her son a meaningful look. "And she's not going to want to stick around, Joe, if you can't make an effort to treat her the way she deserves to be treated."

Joe stood up, his boots heavy on the floor. "Fine. We'll go out, do something, even though we're perfectly happy being here—"

"Sophie," Mrs. Wyatt interrupted, "are you happy being here, every night, all the time?"

Sophie's mouth opened, closed. She glanced at Joe and then back to his mom. "Joe's right. I am a homebody," she answered carefully.

"You don't like going to dinner, or out to hear music? You wouldn't enjoy listening to live music at Grey's?"

When Sophie didn't immediately answer, Mrs. Wyatt continued, "Just realize you're setting a precedent now. You're setting expectations for the future. If Joe thinks he never needs to take you out, if he thinks you don't enjoy a date night, or being treated special, then you'll be sitting in this room every night for the rest of your life." She gave Sophie a meaningful look. "I've spent the twenty-six past years in this room, night after night. If you can get out, and you'd like to get out, do it. Make Joe spoil you. Every woman should be spoiled now and then."

THERE WAS NO staying in after that. Joe and Sophie changed and, grabbing their coats, headed out to Joe's truck, dogs running ahead of them.

They didn't talk for the first five minutes, and then exchanged only a few words when Joe turned down the radio to ask if she was warm enough. Sophie replied that she was fine.

They drove for another ten minutes, and then Joe sighed and turned the radio off. "This is not going to be a fun date night," he said curtly.

"No, it's not. Maybe we should go back."

He made a low, rough sound deep in his chest. "And deal with my mom? No, thank you."

The corner of Sophie's mouth lifted. "She looks so delicate, too."

"Yeah. Looks are deceiving." He shot Sophie a side glance. "You women are ruthless when you want to be."

"We women? What about you men? You can be impossible."

He pulled off the road, taking an exit that led to an old

building and empty parking lot. Joe parked in the lot, turned
the engine off, and faced her. "Do you know what's impossible? Thinking this would be a comfortable and practical
relationship. I don't regret picking you, but it's not comfortable or practical."

"I've been nothing but practical. Whatever you want, I'll
do—"

"Now you're just torturing me."

"How?"

"Girl, all I want is you. And you're the one thing I can't
have."

She huffed a shocked laugh. "What are you talking
about? We're married. I'm your wife. You have me."

"Not where I want you," he growled, the sound deep and
husky and distinctively male.

The sexy rasp in his voice made her heart race. "Where
do you want me?"

"Under me, on top of me, next to me, against me."

Sophie's cheeks burned hot and her lips parted in a silent
gasp.

"Nothing?" he said. "Have I shocked you?"

"No," she whispered. "Not shocked. Maybe surprised."

"Surprised?"

"I know we have some chemistry when we kiss—"

"This isn't chemistry. This is insanity. I think about you,
and making love to you, twenty-four seven. I shower three
times a day just to try to deal with how much I want you. It

doesn't help that you sleep down the hall from me, and give me such chaste little kisses, but I don't want your chaste little kisses. I want more. I want you."

"Then take more." Her voice cracked. "Take me."

"Take you?" he repeated, voice rough and low. "Don't tease. I'm close to losing my mind."

"Can't have that," she said, unbuckling her seat belt and slipping from her seat to settle onto his lap. She was facing him, her hands resting on his big silver belt buckle. "Don't want to make you crazy. Things are complicated enough as they are."

In the dark, Joe's eyes searched hers, and then he dropped his head and his mouth covered hers in a slow, hungry kiss that sent electric darts of feeling from her mouth to her breasts, and from her breasts to her belly and beyond. He reached up to clasp the back of her head, angling his mouth closer to better taste her.

Sophie rocked forward, pressing her chest to his, craving the friction of his denim covered erection against her inner thighs.

Joe's tongue swept her mouth, stirring tiny nerve endings, and reminding her how it felt to have a man want her, love her. And maybe Joe didn't love her, but his kiss made her feel alive and beautiful. His kiss made her hum and shiver with need.

She'd thought she'd never feel this way again. She thought she'd lost the chance to be wanted, desired, cherished and yet this new husband of hers was kissing her senseless, turning her body—and heart—inside out.

Suddenly, Sophie couldn't get close enough, and she wrapped her arms around his neck, pressing herself to him, welcoming the hard planes of his big muscular body against her softness. And just when Sophie thought he'd unbutton her blouse or unzip her jeans, he drew back and stared into her eyes.

"What do you want, Sophie?" he asked, cradling her warm, flushed face between his hands. "What do you want from me?"

Her pulse thudded so hard. She fought to catch her breath. "I want you to want me."

"I do. What else?"

She took another breath, trying to steady her racing pulse. "I want you to like me."

"I like you so much it's got me tied up in knots."

"Don't be in knots. I like you, too. A whole lot."

"Do you now?"

"Yeah," she said, smiling into his eyes, and tugging on a strand of his crisp straight hair.

"What else do you want?" he asked.

She shrugged. "I don't have a list of demands, Joe. I want you happy, and I want to be happy, too. I'm hoping we can be happy together."

"What did you want from Leo?"

She shook her head, uncomfortable. "It's in the past. It

doesn't matter."

"Not that far in the past. It was just December."

She leaned against Joe's chest, his body so warm she wanted to get lost in him. "I thought I was in a forever relationship," she said slowly. "But it wasn't. And I lost faith in me, and I lost faith in him. I guess the part that still bothers me is that I didn't see the end coming. I didn't see that there were problems." Her shoulders lifted and fell. "But maybe I didn't want to see the problems. Maybe that's why I'm cautious with you. I want us to be the real thing. I want us to work, to last."

"We will. That's a promise." Joe gathered her long hair back from her face and neck, and pressed a kiss beneath her ear. She shivered, and he kissed her again, a little lower, on the side of her neck where she was sensitive. Sophie arched and sighed, unable to hide her pleasure.

And then his hands were under her blouse, his palms so warm against her skin, sending streaks of dizzying sensation throughout her body. It had been months since she'd been touched, months since she'd felt attractive or desirable. As his hands caressed over her stomach and up toward her ribs, his knuckles brushed the underside of her breasts and that light, fleeting touch made the air catch in her throat, and her pulse drum in her veins.

When he stroked her through her bra, she whimpered at the pleasure.

Suddenly a bright white light shone through the back

window of the truck, and focused on them, blinding Sophie. She lifted a hand to shield her eyes.

Joe swore beneath his breath. "It's either a ranger or a sheriff," he muttered, lifting her back onto her seat and tugging her top down before adjusting himself.

Sure enough, a uniformed deputy approached the truck, his flashlight swinging, checking out the interior of the truck cab.

Joe rolled the truck window down. "Logan," he said, greeting the deputy sheriff. "How's it going?"

"Good. How are you, Joe?" the deputy said, trying to look severe but failing. "Everything okay, here?"

"Everything's fine," Joe answered.

"Truck didn't break down?" Logan asked.

"No. We're just trying to get a little alone time." Joe gestured to Sophie. "Have you met my fiancée yet, Sophie Correia?"

"I haven't." The deputy extended his hand through the window to Sophie. "Logan Tate."

"Nice to meet you, Logan."

"Same," Logan said, before glancing at Joe. "When's the wedding?"

"A couple weeks," Joe said gruffly. "It'll be at Emerson's Barn. You should come."

"Send me an invite and I will."

CHAPTER NINE

S OPHIE GIGGLED AS Joe started the truck and they headed back onto the highway heading for Marietta. "That was embarrassing," she said, "but also funny. I don't think I've been caught making out in a car since I was a junior in high school."

"I just found it embarrassing," Joe answered. "I've known Logan Tate forever, and I don't need him playing sheriff with me."

"He seemed to think it was funny, too."

"Because he's a deputy sheriff."

"Do you have an issue with authority figures, Joe Wyatt?"

"No. Just Logan." He smiled reluctantly. "He and I used to go at it."

"Fight?"

"*All* the time."

"Why?"

"Don't know why. I guess it's what boys do."

"To establish dominance," Sophie said. "I know how this works. I have brothers. But there had to be a reason you and

Logan would get into it that frequently."

"I actually don't remember. I know I used to be more of a hothead. I was angry about a lot of things. Dad dying. Mom falling apart. Granddad being Granddad."

"What does that mean?"

"Granddad used to be a lot harder. He's mellowed over the years, especially when we all left to compete on the PRCA circuit. But when we were kids, he was strict, and he didn't put up with any backtalk. Heaven help you if he caught you rolling your eyes."

"Would he hit you?"

"No, but he'd give you chores from dawn to dusk. The worst chores. Usually involving, mud, muck, and manure. When we arrived here after my dad died, we didn't know what hit us. We were pretty torn up, at least I know I was, and I didn't want to be in Montana. I didn't want to be stuck on that ranch. And I didn't want my mom crying all the time. I was angry, and I took my frustration out on the playground. I'd look for trouble. I loved to fight. But then, we all did. Sam, Billy, Tommy, me—we were our own wild pack. Scrappy. A lot of the other ranching families in the valley weren't fans of ours. They complained about us to the school, they complained about us to Granddad, they complained about us to anyone who'd listen. I guess we were hoodlums." His lips twisted and he shook his head. "That's when Granddad got us involved in the junior rodeo. It's hard to have the energy to fight if you're always sore and nursing broken bones from riding, roping, and wrestling steers."

It was the longest Sophie had ever heard him talk about anything, and the most words she'd ever heard him say at one time, and it crossed her mind again that he kept so much inside. He must have a whole world of hurt and grief locked down within him. And for the first time, she understood that him getting over Charity probably had less to do with Charity herself and more to do with loss in general. His not dating wasn't because he couldn't find another woman as wonderful as Charity, but that his heart couldn't handle more pain.

"Sounds like you Wyatt boys took to the junior rodeo pretty well," she said, putting her hand on his leg, just above his knee. "I saw some of your impressive buckles in your room. Your mom said there's a lot more that you just dumped in a box and put away."

"I had a good run there."

"You couldn't compete still? Not even at some pro-am type events?"

"Maybe. But unless the event was close to home, it wouldn't make sense to do it. It's just hard to leave the ranch. I can do it for a day, but a whole weekend? Not fair to Granddad."

"You couldn't hire more ranch hands? You've got a couple."

"I actually meant I couldn't leave my mom's care to Granddad. It's not fair to him." He hesitated. "I've thought a lot about hiring Mom some help. It will probably be necessary down the road—"

"I can help her, Joe."

"You're not here to be a nurse, and I appreciate you offering, but that's a definite no. It's hard being a caretaker, and we're going to have kids, and they'll have activities, and you're going to need a life, too."

She rubbed her palm across his knee, the denim smooth, his body warm. "What about you?" she asked. "Don't you need a life?"

His hand covered hers. His voice dropped, deepening, "Thanks to you, Sophie, I've now got one."

IT WAS COLD when they stepped out of the truck on Main Street and walked to Grey's Saloon, the wind an icy blast. Joe glanced up at the sky. Clouds had gathered, obscuring the moon. The weather had changed dramatically since this morning. He hadn't paid attention to the weather report today, but he should have. He had a feeling temperatures were going to keep dropping and that wouldn't be good with all the heifers ready to calve.

Part of him wanted to go home and check in on the pregnant cows they'd brought to the pasture nearest the house, and another part of him felt like he owed Sophie a drink and a night out. They didn't have to stay out long, either. Just one beer, listen to a little music, and head home.

They found a table not far from the jukebox and they ordered drinks but Joe's mind was elsewhere. Seeing Logan, talking about being a kid, remembering all the trouble he used to get in had stirred other memories, memories not as comfortable. Mom hadn't been herself for years after they arrived in Montana. She hadn't taken to bed, but she was numb. Shut down. She was there physically, but not emotionally, and some of Joe's antics were to get his mom's attention, and somehow make her love him again. He knew now that she hadn't ever stopped loving him, or his brothers, but her grief was so big, and so consuming, she couldn't be there for the boys. There was a stretch of time—four years, five—where she was just gone, and Granddad was doing everything for them, literally everything, and then his grandfather insisted his mother get counseling. Mom had been resistant but counseling helped, and she came back to them, little by little. Maybe that was why Joe was so glad to see her enjoying the wedding planning. He still remembered when she didn't smile. He still remembered when she just sat at the kitchen table as if a marble statue.

"Hey," Sophie said, extending a hand to him. "I'm Sophie Correia, and I'm new to Marietta. Who are you?"

He smiled and took her hand, giving it a shake. "Joe Wyatt. Nice to meet you, Sophie. How are you liking Montana?"

"I like it. A lot."

"Yeah?"

"Pretty state. Handsome cowboys."

"You like cowboys?"

"Now I do," she said.

"Anything else I should know? We've never discussed politics."

"And I don't think we need to. Politics remind me of faith. You have your views, I have mine, and we're not going to try to convert the other."

The corner of his mouth briefly lifted. "I have faith."

"Good, me, too."

"And I'm an American."

"Me, too."

"I love this country."

"As do I," Sophie answered, grinning back at him.

She was so dang cute. Big brown eyes, soft full mouth, a heart-shaped face. He could get lost in those eyes, and kiss that mouth for hours. There was a lot of things he wanted to do, and would do, when the time was ready.

He was ready.

She was the one not yet ready.

He sensed it had to do with Leo and the wedding that didn't happen. Joe felt like there was more to the story.

He reached out and took her hand. "I know we've only been here a half hour, but I'm worried about the weather and some things I haven't taken care of at the ranch. Would you mind if we finished this beer and headed back?"

"Not at all. I've got work tomorrow and I'm tired. I'm

not used to fighting with you."

"I hate fighting with you, but let's face it, we're not going to always see eye to eye, and I like that you can hold your own with me. Don't ever feel like you can't be yourself. I don't expect you to be a parrot. I can be tough, and blunt, and sometimes difficult to please, but that's not on you. That's on me. It's not your job to make me happy. It's my job to make me happy. Got it?"

She leaned across the table and kissed him. "Got it. Now let's go home."

SOPHIE SHIVERED AS they walked quickly back to his truck, the icy whistling wind pushing them forward. "It's freezing," she said, teeth chattering. "And just two days ago it was really warm."

"Montana weather for you," Joe said, unlocking the truck.

She glanced up at the sky, squinting as if she could read something in the darkness before hopping into the truck. "Can you imagine the poor couple getting married tomorrow? You'd think it's winter again."

"Montanans expect bad weather. The good weather is a gift." As he reversed out of the angled spot and then shifted into drive, he glanced at her. "And you're a gift."

For a moment, Sophie didn't know what to say. "Thank you."

"I mean it. I'm glad you're here, and I hope you're happy—"

"I am, Joe, and I know it's all still new and we're both adjusting, but considering its only been a month since I arrived, I think we're doing well."

"I hope so."

She cocked her head. "You have doubts?"

"I just know how much warmth you've brought to the ranch. Everything is just brighter, more hopeful. I'm more hopeful—"

"Good!" She leaned across the console and kissed his cheek. "That makes me happy."

"We need you, Sophie." His voice dropped. "I need you."

"Well, you have me."

"Not all of you," he said, shooting her a look, his blue gaze intense. "But hopefully, soon."

THE HOUSE WAS dark when they arrived, and Mrs. Wyatt and Granddad were in bed. Even the dogs were too tired to get up and bark. Thankfully, the kitchen was still warm, and Sophie hung up her coat, and headed to the stove to put on the teakettle. "I'm going to make a cup of tea to take to bed with me. Want one?"

He shook his head. "I'd rather take you to bed with me."

"We could," she said, reaching for a mug. "If it made

you feel better." She knew immediately that wasn't the right thing to say. Joe's jaw hardened and his brow furrowed. "Sorry, that didn't come out quite the way I meant it."

"How did you mean it? Because everything you do turns me on and yet I get the feeling that you're not sure about me."

Suddenly, there was a spike in tension and Sophie only had herself to blame. "Sex is just going to be weird for me the first time. Maybe I shouldn't say it that way, but you're going to be the first person I've been with since Leo—"

"Oh, how I hate Leo."

"Joe!"

"Just saying."

"And before Leo, there wasn't anyone else. He was my first. I don't really have a lot of experience beyond Leo, and therefore not a lot of confidence—"

"Let's just hope I don't ever meet him. I'd—"

"*No,*" she said, cutting him off before he could say anything incriminating. "Leo's not worth your time or energy. You don't have to hate him. I don't hate Charity."

"Totally different situation."

"How?"

"First of all, Charity was always honest with me. I knew when we started dating that she was someone raised in town, who loved living in town. Not everyone's cut out for the ranch life, and she wasn't."

"But you guys got serious."

"Yes, and for a long time we tried to make it work, but in the end, she wouldn't have been happy on the ranch, and we both knew it. It would have been too lonely for her, too removed from her family and friends."

"Even with your mom here?" Sophie asked.

"Yes," he said simply. "I hated letting her go, but it was the right thing to do."

"Did you ever get back together?"

"Many times, but then we'd break up again, and each breakup got harder. Each goodbye hurt more. During our final breakup we agreed to never call, email, or reach out to the other again. We vowed to never see each other again. And that was the end of it. Finally."

The heaviness in his voice made her ache for him. "That had to have been hard."

"Beyond hard."

"And then when you decided you needed to move on, you vowed not to fall in love again, didn't you?"

He shot her a sharp glance. "I vowed to find someone more independent, more self-sufficient. Someone who could be happy here. And I found you."

"Through an ad."

"But it worked."

"We were both trying to be practical," she said, using a hot pad to remove the whistling teakettle from the burner. "We wanted a mature, businesslike arrangement. No emotions involved."

"Not sure we've been successful there. I'm finding it next to impossible not to feel things for you."

Sophie lifted her head, looked at him. "Is that so?"

"You know it's so. I can't keep my hands off of you."

She held her smile, but inwardly her heart sank a little. He wanted her body. She wanted his heart. This definitely was more complicated than she'd imagined, because sex and love weren't the same thing, but hopefully physical need could lead to other things... like love.

Hopefully.

"It's late," Joe said suppressing a yawn. "I'm going to be up early tomorrow. I suppose we should call it a night."

Sophie picked up her steaming mug and Joe turned out the kitchen light. On the second floor outside Sophie's room, Joe said, "Sunday it'll be two weeks until wedding number two. We will survive until then?"

"I think so." She stood up on tiptoe and kissed him, careful not to slosh her tea. "Good night, Joe."

"Good night, Sophie. Sleep tight."

SOPHIE DIDN'T SEE Joe Saturday morning before she headed into town to work. The weather had turned in the night, temperatures plummeting even lower. It began to rain as she drove down the mountain, and halfway down, the rain turned to a slushy sleet. She turned her windshield wipers up and cranked on her heater. It had been beautiful two days ago and now it felt like winter.

By noon, the rain turned to snow, and Sophie watched the fat flakes fall, jaw dropping in awe. She went to the big window in the salon to watch the snow tumble from the sky. It was beyond beautiful. She'd never lived anyplace where it snowed.

Amanda joined her briefly at the window. "Let me guess. Your first snow."

"It's magical," Sophie breathed.

"Yes, but it's also May second. We're all getting a little sick of it."

"But look, it's so pretty. Everything is turning white."

Amanda smiled and returned to her station. "We'll see how you feel next January."

The afternoon flew by. Sophie had expected a lot of cancellations due to the snow but no one cancelled. If anything, the phone wouldn't stop ringing with clients asking about last-minute availability. But the day was over and Sophie was in the middle of closing the salon when Joe called. "It's finally stopped snowing here," he said. "How is it in town?"

"A beautiful powdery white," she said. "Joe, there's snow everywhere."

He laughed. "I wondered if you'd be excited or terrified."

"I love it. It's so beautiful."

"Be careful driving. Make sure you're in four-wheel drive. Take it slow. No need to hurry."

"I will. See you in a bit."

Sophie hummed the whole way home, feeling giddy, and buoyant. The dogs raced out to greet her and she didn't stiffen quite as much. She even managed to pat a few big heads before disappearing into the house. She peeled off her coat and hung it on the hook by the back door but stopped when she heard Joe and his grandfather talking. Their conversation sounded serious, something about two more calves lost, and how they had to be extra vigilant tomorrow.

Sophie entered the kitchen just as Granddad walked out. Joe was still leaning against the kitchen counter, arms folded over his chest. He'd recently showered, his brown hair was dark and wet, but he was wearing a heavy sweater over his shirt, and he had boots on again. He smiled when he saw her but his smile didn't reach his eyes.

"Bad day?" she asked.

"Frustrating. Winter weather can be disastrous during calving season. I should have been paying more attention. I'm heading back out now. I probably won't be back until late."

"Can I make you anything?"

"I already grabbed a bite. Don't wait up for me tonight."

"Is there anything I can do?"

"No." He approached, kissed her, and headed for the door, grabbing his hat and coat on the way. "Glad you're home safe."

"Be careful."

"Yep."

❦

Joe was out all day Sunday again, and late Sunday night. He came in exhausted, and Sophie reheated a bowl of the beef burgundy she'd tried to make for dinner. It wasn't as good as she'd hoped, the chunks of meat had been cut too small and had cooked down to nothing, but Joe didn't seem to notice. He wolfed down the meat and egg noodles and then yawned. "Thank you, I needed that."

"You must be beat," she said.

"I am pretty tired." He stood, stretched, and then remembered something. "Aren't we supposed to cake test tomorrow?"

"Yes."

"Is there any way I can get out of it?"

"Yes! Great idea. I'm happy to cancel. We can just order a cake without—"

"Actually, Mom would love to go with you," he interrupted. "And then you two were going to look at dresses? You could just do both with her. If you don't mind."

Sophie hid her disappointment, because she understood, and truthfully, she knew Mrs. Wyatt would enjoy a day out. "I don't mind."

"Are you sure?"

"Yes."

"It's going to be icy. Mom won't be stable on her feet."

"I'll keep a tight grip on her. Won't let her fall."

❦

JOE WAS ALREADY gone in the morning when Sophie woke up, and Mrs. Wyatt, who usually slept in until midmorning, was up early as well. Joe was right. She was excited about going into town and having a day doing wedding things together.

The cake tasting went well. Mrs. Wyatt really enjoyed the experience, stretching the forty-five minute appointment at Cake Art by Gabby into ninety minutes, but Gabby had no other appointments until later that day and she answered all of Mrs. Wyatt's questions, and even brought out a few other cake flavors and fillings for them to sample. In the end, they went with the cake combination Mrs. Wyatt said Joe liked best—white layer cake with chocolate mousse filling.

They also discussed the design for the three tiers and Sophie said she would be happy with anything simple and decorated with a few clusters of fresh flowers. Mrs. Wyatt pulled out her folder with the ideas she'd torn from magazines and showed the pictures. "I don't know if you could include a burlap ribbon around the base, or something else rustic. As you know, the wedding is at the Emerson Barn and it's rustic chic."

Sophie almost laughed out loud when she heard Joe's mom describe the wedding theme, but it wasn't an unkind laugh. In some ways, Sophie was charmed. Mrs. Wyatt was enjoying the wedding plans far more than Sophie's mother ever did.

They left the cake tasting and headed to Married in

Marietta with Mrs. Wyatt in high spirits despite the obstacles of getting to the parked Jeep through piles of dirty, slushy snow in the gutter and mounded on street corners.

During the short drive to the bridal store, Mrs. Wyatt said that they'd have to choose something that was in stock as there was no time to order anything custom at this point. "However, they've assured me the seamstress can alter anything to make it fit you. We just need to find a gown that thrills you."

Sophie parked in front of Married in Marietta and turned off the engine. "I think I should prepare you that it's unlikely I'll find anything that thrills me. If we can find something simple, and inexpensive—"

"Why do you do that? Why keep insisting everything be inexpensive? It takes the fun away."

Sophie turned to face her mother-in-law. She didn't want to hurt her feelings, but Sophie was struggling, truly struggling. "Mrs. Wyatt—"

"Maybe it's time you call me Summer?" Joe's mom looked up at her and smiled. "Mrs. Wyatt sounds so old, and I know I'm all arthritic, but hopefully I don't look as old as I feel on the inside."

There was something so earnest and almost girlish in Mrs. Wyatt's expression that Sophie's heart turned over. She couldn't bear upsetting her mother-in-law, and yet Sophie thought she'd explode if she continued keeping all her emotions and secrets and worries in. Joe was wonderful in his way, but he wasn't the easiest to talk to. He wanted to solve problems, not listen to problems, and what Sophie really needed now, was someone to just listen.

"Mrs. Wyatt—" Sophie broke off, swallowed, and tried again. "Summer, I have to tell you something. I probably should have told you this before, but this wedding planning is hard for me." She paused and glanced at Joe's mom. "It's not just the money, but that's part of it. It's also the planning itself, and the discussion of all the details, from cake to wedding gown. It probably shouldn't still cause me so much pain. You'd think by now I'd be okay with it." She stopped talking, and searched her mother-in-law's face but could see Summer didn't understand. She wasn't following.

"I was supposed to get married last year," Sophie said quietly, not wanting to give away too much about the end of her relationship with Leo and the start of her relationship with Joe, but also desperate to make this terrible awkwardness go away. "A few days before the wedding, my fiancé broke it off. I thought then that maybe he had cold feet. I thought we might get back together. I actually believed that our wedding was still going to go on as planned—and then he called me and confessed that he was in love with someone else."

The silence in the car was deafening. Sophie was so incredibly uncomfortable. She had no idea what Summer was thinking, but at least it was out there in the open. "It's not that I don't want a nice wedding with Joe. It's not that he doesn't deserve one. It's just that I—" Sophie's voice cracked and tears filled her eyes. "I don't think I do." One tear fell, and then another, and she wiped them fiercely, swiftly away. "And so, please don't think I'm ungrateful when I know you're trying so hard to be helpful, but in my heart I feel… wrong… letting this wedding happen this way, and feel even worse spending money after all the money my mom spent last December."

"You couldn't probably get any of that money back, could you?"

"No."

"Your mother probably spent a fortune."

"She did."

"You blame yourself," Summer added.

Sophie nodded. "I do."

"But he was the one to walk away, not you, and now you're marrying Joe, aren't you?"

"Yes," Sophie whispered.

"You're starting a new life together."

Sophie dashed away another tear and nodded.

"So what part causes you pain? The starting a new life with Joe, or—"

"Not the new life with Joe. I love Joe." And then she blushed and fell silent as she realized what she'd just said.

She loved Joe.

And as impossible as it all seemed, she did.

Summer reached out and clasped Sophie gently on the

forearm. "So the part that gives you pain is the wedding?"

"Yes."

Summer gave Sophie another little squeeze. "But isn't what you're having more of a party? You and Joe have already decided you want to say your vows in private with Revered Rowe. All the guests are being invited to the reception. That's different from what you were doing in California, isn't it?"

"Yes."

"And I don't know all the circumstances around your engagement in California, but I know this, you and Joe should celebrate the start of your new life together. I think you're both very special."

Fresh tears stung Sophie's eyes. "I didn't think you liked me."

"I wasn't a fan of him meeting someone online, but you've grown on me." Summer smiled almost mischievously. "Quite a bit."

"You'll be okay with me as your daughter-in-law?"

"I'm delighted to have you as my daughter-in-law."

"Thank you." She wiped away one last tear. "You give really good advice."

"In that case, can I give you one more bit of advice?"

"Of course."

"Let yourself be happy, Sophie. Don't you think it's time?"

Inside the store, Summer settled into an armchair in the

corner. "Let's see you try some dresses on. I want you to model four or five of your favorites for me, and before you march to the discount rack, or suggest we visit a thrift store, you should know that is not happening. Joe is my oldest. He was my first baby. His bride is going to look like a proper bride." Summer's expression softened. "You will be such a beautiful bride, too. We just need the right dress."

It wasn't all that long ago that Sophie had tried on dozens of bridal gowns. She knew which kind of design flattered her figure. She was too short and too curvy to wear the princess ball gown look. She needed something simple, as well as something classic, and fitted, and so she flicked through the gowns in the big garment bags, but nothing really appealed. She felt as if she'd done all of this before, and had tried on a million dresses before. The truth was, she didn't want to wear a bridal gown. She didn't want to wear white at all.

Sophie left the bridal gown section and walked over to the bridesmaid dresses and flicked through pale pink gowns and peach gowns. She looked at light gray gowns and then the light blue gowns and stopped when she found one that was light blue. She didn't love the cheap satin fabric bodice, but the lace overlay on the skirt reminded her of the lace on the wedding invitations and the price tag said it was less than one hundred dollars and the blue reminded her of Joe's eyes.

"What about this one?" she said, turning around to show Summer.

Summer just looked at her, obviously not impressed. "Why that one?"

"The blue reminds me of Joe's eyes." She smiled. "He has gorgeous eyes."

"His dad had the same shade of blue." Summer drew a breath. "His dad was very handsome and very kind. He was truly chivalrous. I loved him madly."

"Is that why you never married again?"

"There was only one man for me, and that was my JC." Summer cleared her throat, and shifted her cane. "Let's get the sales girl over. I like your idea of a blue gown, but surely we can do better than that one."

CHAPTER TEN

T HEY DID DO better than that one. They found a gorgeous dress with a fitted lace bodice, long lace sleeves, and a full tulle skirt, and while the dress was white, the owner of the bridal salon promised that it could be dyed the perfect light, dusty-blue shade.

Summer loved the dress, and it fit Sophie well without too many alterations. It would need to be hemmed, and the sleeves shortened an inch, but it fit her everywhere else.

"Do you really like it?" Summer asked anxiously. "I don't want you to pick this one because you think I like it—"

"I love it. It's nothing like the dress I would have worn to marry Leo. It's nothing like anything I've ever worn, but it's rather perfect for our rustic chic wedding in the Emerson Barn."

"Now you're teasing me," Summer said.

"Maybe a little." Sophie leaned forward and hugged her mother-in-law. "Thank you for spending today with me. I enjoyed myself."

"Me, too."

"HOW DID IT go?" Joe asked when they arrived home later that afternoon. "You were out all day."

"Good," Sophie said brightly. "It was fun."

Joe's brow lifted. "Fun?"

She nodded. "Your mom must be exhausted, though. I am," Sophie said, giving him a hug even as she flashed Summer a smile. "But we got so much done despite the mess the roads were in. It's so dirty everywhere."

"Not the pristine-white snow you loved on Saturday," Joe said.

"No," she agreed. "But we have a cake ordered, a dress purchased, and a check cut to the caterers."

Joe's mom settled into a chair at the kitchen table. "We also had lunch at a cute little place downtown. Java something. Nice sandwiches and salads."

"And then we stopped by Emerson's Barn on the way home so I could see it for myself," Sophie concluded. "It's really nice. Thinking that we should have the whole reception inside, though. It'd be warmer, and more comfortable for women wearing party dresses."

"You really did cover it all," he said, impressed.

"How was your day?"

"We didn't lose any calves today, and the weather's warming. We should be up fifteen degrees by Thursday, and almost balmy this weekend."

"That's such a crazy change in weather."

"That's Montana," Summer said with a weary smile.

"You know, I think I might just go to bed early. I'm more tired than I thought."

"How about I make you something light to eat?" Sophie offered. "I'd hate for you to go to bed without any dinner."

"I don't need dinner, not after all that cake today. I think a cup of tea would be nice and I'll just turn in."

"I'll make the tea," Sophie offered.

"I'll help you upstairs, Mom," Joe said.

THE NEXT FEW days passed in a flurry of work, wedding preparations, normal life errands, dinner prep, and dishes. Sophie's head buzzed with all there was to do, and the wedding that she hadn't wanted, actually became exciting and part of her wished she'd invited her family. Part of her wanted them here to meet Joe so they'd know just how wonderful he was.

Thursday evening, after work, she was in the barn with Joe admiring the calf that had been born that morning and admiring the calf had turned into a stolen make-out session. They kissed until they were breathless and then Sophie giggled and he asked why she laughed, and she said she kept waiting for the deputy sheriff to arrive and tell them to knock it off.

Joe laughed, too, and they kissed as they laughed and Sophie pulled her phone out of her back pocket and snapped a selfie of them together. "I think this is our first picture together," she said, smiling into the camera with Joe's handsome face just above hers, his strong arms wrapped around her. She took another quick couple of pics, and then put the phone away because Joe was kissing her neck, and then kissing her collarbone, and she turned in his arms, and melted against him, boneless, mindless to all, but the pleasure.

It wasn't until later that night, when she was in bed, she remembered the photos and she pulled out her phone to look at the three selfies. They were smiling in each and they looked good together. Happy together.

She looked happy.

Sophie zoomed in on the photo and studied her face, but mostly her eyes, and they were shining, bright with joy, and love. So much love.

And now she and Joe were marrying again, in just ten days, and this time it wasn't because it was practical, but because it was fun. It would be a party. A wonderful party because they'd be celebrating their future.

Impulsively she sent one of the pics in a group text to her family. "*Found my heart in Montana. Marrying Joe Wyatt next Sunday. Can't wait for you all to meet him.*"

Sophie woke up to a dozen texts from her large family, some with questions, others congratulating her. Her mother was concerned, fearing Sophie hadn't thought it through, and would regret her decision. Her oldest brother wanted her to know if he should fly out and meet this guy. Another brother, the lawyer, said he looked into Joe Wyatt and he didn't have a record, if that was useful. Sarah sent a text with just a red heart emoji.

Sophie answered each that she was good, and for no one to worry, and she promised to come to California sometime with Joe so everyone could meet him. And then she showered, dressed, made a quick breakfast before heading into Marietta for work.

It proved to be a hectic Friday. The salon was crowded, with every stylist booked all day, with the phone ringing frequently with last minute calls from clients hoping to get in Friday or Saturday. The weather had done a one-eighty from two weeks ago and was blissfully sunny and bright, with temperatures predicted to be in the high seventies all weekend. Sophie hoped the good weather would hold for another week. She'd love weather like this for her and Joe's barn wedding next Sunday.

SUNDAY WAS MOTHER'S Day and Sophie had surprised the Wyatts by making a reservation at the Graff Hotel for their Mother's Day brunch. She cornered Joe and Melvin in the barn and let them know about her plans. "I know you don't all normally go into town for brunch, but I've heard they do an amazing buffet and they have fresh flowers for the moms and I think Summer should be spoiled."

"That's a long way to go just for food," Melvin answered.

"It's not just food, Granddad," she answered. "It's really good food and it's a chance for Summer to look pretty and go out and be seen with her family. Women like that sort of thing, and she doesn't get to do enough of it here."

"Mom never asks to go out," Joe said.

"Because she's outnumbered. But she's not outnumbered anymore. She's got backup now, and we're going to make her feel special today. Our reservation is for eleven. We should leave by ten, just so she can take her time getting from the car to the dining room."

"Does Mom know?" Joe asked.

Sophie smiled. "I'm going to take her a cup of coffee and tell her our plans now."

Summer was surprised by the Mother's Day brunch plans, and halfheartedly argued against a trip to town, but when Sophie told her that Joe and Granddad would probably love the buffet featuring a carving station with roast beef and a honey glazed ham, Summer caved, agreeing that it did sound like a lovely treat.

At the Graff, they were seated at a table for four not far from the table where Sophie and Joe had sat on the day of their courthouse wedding ceremony. She glanced at Joe, wondering if he remembered, and he smiled. "Our table," he mouthed.

She grinned, delighted. Even better, the Wyatts all seemed to enjoy the lavish brunch, with Summer sending Joe back for seconds for her from the dessert table, while Joe and

Grandad had seconds and then thirds from the carving station. Sophie ate a little bit of everything, from the omelet to the salads to the fancy shrimp on ice. She sampled one of the tiny lemon meringue tarts, as well as a pretty pink petit four.

The dining room manager walked around the room passing out roses to all the mothers in the room. Summer blushed and thanked the manager for her long stem rose. "This was such a wonderful idea. Thank you, family," she said, eyes bright. "I don't even wish your brothers were here because I'm hoping they'll show up next Sunday for the wedding."

"And if they can't," Joe said, "we'll still have a wonderful day. Next weekend, there's big prize money out there. I fully expect the boys to be chasing the money."

WHEN NO ONE could eat another bite, or wanted another splash of coffee, Joe signaled for the bill. The waiter approached and quietly let him know that the bill had already been taken care of. Joe glanced at Sophie, who was smiling, and looking impossibly pleased with herself.

"This is my gift to all of you," she said.

She'd always been pretty, and she'd always been optimistic, but in that moment she was downright radiant, lighting the room with her beautiful, generous heart. He felt impossibly lucky, and improbably lucky, to have met her online.

They were on their way out, walking through the historic hotel's lobby, when Sophie suddenly clutched his arm. "She's here," Sophie whispered, clearly panicked.

"Who?" Joe asked, his gaze sweeping the lobby with the columns, dark paneling, and polished marble floor.

"Sarah." Sophie's voice cracked. "My sister is here."

Everyone had stopped walking, and they were all looking at her. "Is that a bad thing?" he asked, bewildered.

"Yes."

"Why?"

She shook her head, eyes wide and luminous in her starkly pale face. "I can't do this," she choked. "I can't do this here—"

"We'll just all walk on out," his mom said. "We'll just keep going."

Joe wanted to ask Sophie what was going on, but his mom gave him a sharp look and he took her elbow again and continued escorting her out.

They waited on the curb while valet brought their car around, and Sophie stared out the window, heartsick, during the drive home. It wasn't until they were back on the ranch that Sophie sought Joe out to speak to him alone.

"Remember how I told you that my fiancé broke off the engagement with me, just days before the wedding?" she said, her voice faint and unsteady.

He nodded, his gaze riveted to her pale face.

She chewed her lip for a moment and then blurted, "Leo

ended things with me because he was in love with my sister Sarah. Two months later, Leo and Sarah married on Valentine's Day."

No wonder she'd been so heartsick. "That's why you wanted to get away from your family."

She nodded. "It wasn't just Leo I lost. I lost them... all of them. My family embraced Leo. They accepted him into the family as if nothing had happened. I just felt so betrayed. I felt like I had no family."

"Which is why Montana appealed."

She nodded again. "I wanted to get away. I wanted to start over. And thanks to you, I have."

"And your sister is here now."

"With Leo," she added, her voice nearly inaudible.

"What?"

"I suspect she's worried about me. She's been calling, trying to make amends—"

"And you're not taking her calls."

"But why would she bring Leo to Marietta with her? Why would she do that to me?" Tears suddenly filled her eyes. "I don't want to see her. I don't know what to say to her. We were close growing up but I'll never trust her again. Maybe that's harsh, but it's how I feel.

"Sarah was my best friend growing up, but I just feel so betrayed."

"It hasn't been that long, either. It's not even been six months since Leo deserted you."

"Two months since they married."

Joe could feel his temper stirring, his mood darkening. "Have you and Sarah talked at all?"

Sophie hesitated then shook her head. "Not really. I mean, what are we supposed to say? What can she say? She's sorry? So, okay, she's sorry, but Leo wasn't hers. She was free to fall in love with anyone she wanted... just not my man."

Her man.

Joe felt as if he'd just been punched in the gut. His pulse quickened, the anger thick, heavy. "I hope you hold Leo equally responsible."

"Oh, I do. He's not innocent. Not at all."

"And now they've tracked you down to Montana."

"It seems so," she said, blinking back tears. "I wish they hadn't. I don't want to see either of them."

"What if Sarah had come to you on her own? Would you feel differently?"

"I don't know. Maybe. Maybe not. It's just all too raw, too soon." Sophie drew a sharp breath. "I don't want her pity. I'm sick of pity, and sympathy."

"How would she even know to come here?"

"I sent a group text last Monday night with a photo of us, saying that I'd found my heart in Montana and we were getting married this coming Sunday."

"So she's come for the wedding?"

"A week early? I don't think so."

"Then why is she here?"

Her gaze met his, expression deeply troubled. "My gut says they've come to stop the wedding."

"So what do you want to do?" he asked. "Are you going to hide here on the ranch, or face her in town?"

Sophie closed her eyes. "Face her in town."

"When?"

"Today, I guess? I'll text her and see if she's free this afternoon."

"If she is, do you want me to go with you? Could you use backup?"

"Nothing dramatic is going to happen, but yes, it'd be great to have you there. At least that way I won't feel outnumbered."

❦

THE MEETING WITH Sarah didn't go the way Sophie planned. For one, they were meeting in a corner of the Graff lobby. For another, Sophie and Sarah had no opportunity to speak alone together. Leo was glued to Sarah's side, sharing a love seat, holding her hand, or wrapping his hand around the back of her neck, or more annoying, rubbing her neck.

Leo had never once rubbed Sophie's neck, which was fine, because Sophie didn't want or need her neck rubbed, but it was just so weird and so uncomfortable seeing Sarah and Leo together that Sophie couldn't concentrate on the conversation.

"I still don't know what you're doing here," Sophie said

when conversation died and she sensed she was supposed to say something.

"Mom was worried about you," Sarah said. "Everyone's worried about you—"

"Because I'm getting married?" Sophie interrupted. "I would think everyone would be happy for me seeing how hurt I was."

"Maybe that's just it," Sarah said, darting a nervous glance at Joe who was standing behind Sophie's chair. "We don't know Joe, although he seems quite nice, and then we weren't invited to the wedding."

"His mom wanted to invite you," Sophie said tartly, "it was my choice not to."

Sarah sighed. "How do you think that made our mom feel?"

"Mom wouldn't have come anyway. She's terrified of flying, and won't get on a little plane. And you have to get on a little plane." Sophie counted to five, and then ten. "And maybe one day you and I will get past this, Sarah. But if you seriously want to get past this, you need to leave Leo home."

Sarah made a soft gasping sound which made Sophie roll her eyes.

"You are not the injured party here, Sarah—"

"And I'm tired of you being the victim," Sarah cried. "You didn't really love Leo. You were marrying him because it was good for your career—"

"Is that how you've justified your actions?" Sophie interrupted, rising.

Sarah rose, too. "The point is, I love Leo and I'm happy. And you love Joe and you're happy. Can't we please put this behind us? Can't we try to move forward?"

"Is that what you want?"

"Yes!"

"Then fine. We will move forward. I don't enjoy being upset with you, and will work on letting the anger go. Please give everyone my love at home. Tell them you met Joe, and I'm happy and all is good. Okay?"

Sarah nodded tearfully. "Okay. And I do love you, Sophie."

Sophie suppressed her frustration long enough to give her sister a swift hug. "I love you, Sarah. Travel safely."

And then she turned around to walk out, more than ready to escape. She'd thought Joe was right there at her side. But then he was moving the opposite direction, and she knew, a split second before his fist connected with Leo's jaw, what was going to happen.

JOE DIDN'T PUNCH Leo because he lost control. He hit him precisely because he was in control. Leo had it coming, and deserved what he got.

His brothers liked to call him old man, and there were times Joe felt like an old man, but not today. Today, he'd thrown a punch as if he were a prize fighter and he'd knocked Leo down on his back.

Adrenaline still pumping, he looked to Sophie, expecting pride, or possibly approval. Instead, she was horrified.

Disgusted and horrified.

He stepped over Leo, grabbed Sophie's arm, and marched her out of the Graff.

Sophie was nearly incoherent though, babbling questions he wasn't in the mood to answer.

From the moment Joe saw Leo, he knew just who he was dealing with. A rich, spoiled, arrogant know-it-all who didn't give a flying fig for anyone else. Joe couldn't fathom how Sophie had fallen for him, but she had, despite the fact that Leo Brazer was a slimy salesman to the core.

INSIDE JOE'S TRUCK, Sophie fought to calm herself. It took her long minutes before she could even bring herself to speak to Joe. "Why would you hit Leo?" she asked faintly.

"Why wouldn't I hit him? He's an ass. He wronged you in every way imaginable." Joe shot her a sharp look. "Why are you defending him?"

Sophie was exhausted, more than exhausted. It had been so stressful, and so draining, to come face-to-face with Sarah and Leo. "I'm not defending him. But I don't understand why you'd hit him. You hit him hard."

"Good."

"Not good, Joe."

"He stood you up. He left you at the altar. He embarrassed you in front of everyone."

"That was in the past."

"Not in the past, obviously not in the past. You haven't moved on. You haven't gotten over him."

"That's not true. I'm here, I married you; we're together."

His laugh was low and mocking. "Are we together?"

"What does that mean?"

"We still have separate rooms. We haven't made love—"

"Because your mom seems to think—"

"Don't blame this on my mom. This is about you. This is about how you're not ready for anything with me."

She tugged on the decorative button on her sweater. "It took you years to get over Charity," she said lowly.

"This isn't about Charity. This is about you. We've been married almost five weeks, and I appreciate that you've needed to take it slow, but I'm beginning to think there's a bigger problem here, that you haven't been honest with me. You haven't told me the truth."

"When we first met, I wasn't ready to sleep with you. I've never been the girl who can get naked on a first or second date. It takes me a while to get to know people. I mean, I was a virgin when I met Leo, a twenty-four year-old virgin. That has to tell you something."

"A twenty-four year-old virgin," he repeated.

"My family was strict, and conservative."

"Leo knew he was the first?"

"Yes."

Joe muttered an oath under his breath. "That dude is such a dick."

"I appreciate that you haven't rushed me into the physical stuff. I know you've been ready—"

"You're beautiful and sexy and, yes, I want you, but I want you to want me back."

"I do."

"Sophie, I saw how you looked at Leo—"

"I didn't even look at Leo."

"No, you did. You gave him a look that I won't ever forget."

"Maybe it was loathing, Joe. Maybe it was disgust. I don't know what you saw on my face but I can promise you, it wasn't love, or lust."

They didn't speak the rest of the drive home, and didn't speak as they entered the house. The TV was on in the family room but Joe didn't go in.

Instead, he just shouted, "Home." Then he climbed the stairs to the second floor.

Sophie watched him walk away from her, and her heart thudded too hard, making her feel sick. She steeled herself for courage and followed Joe upstairs. He was in his room, door shut. She opened his door without knocking. He was standing at the window staring out.

"I swear, I don't love Leo," she said, closing the door behind her. "You must believe me."

"You were so angry with your sister but you didn't say two words to Leo, and he was your fiance. You should have let him have it. Today was your chance."

"But I have nothing to say to him."

"He treated you terribly."

"I know, but he's in the past. He's behind me. He's not important."

"No?"

"No." She closed the distance between them, standing so close that her pulse quickened and she felt a sizzle of energy and awareness. "You're the one that's important. You're the one I care about."

"Even though I hit him?"

"You were defending my honor," she said, lips curving faintly. "Thank you." Her gaze traveled up, over his broad chest, wide shoulders, to his hard jaw and very firm lips. "I don't think I've ever had anyone take my side, so decisively, before."

"I will always take your side."

"Even against your mom?"

"If that's what you need from me."

"I don't need that of you, and I would hate to drive a wedge between you and her. She's grown on me a lot. I've come to care for her a great deal. Just as I care for you a great deal."

"How much?"

She held up her fingers and showed him a tiny space. "This much."

There was a flicker of amusement in his blue eyes. "I wouldn't call that a great deal. That's more of a tiny deal."

"Maybe I'm not good with measurements."

"Doesn't look like it."

"Not sure how to best say it."

"Then maybe we don't talk."

"What would we do instead?"

"I have a few ideas."

"Perhaps you'd like to show me?" she asked, sounding breathless to her own ears.

"Exactly what I was thinking," he said, head dropping, his mouth covering her as he walked her backward, and pushed her up against the wall. Joe's hands caught hers, and lifted them, pinning her hands by her head, holding her captive.

He kissed her deeply, leaning into her with his weight, a knee between her legs, his chest imprisoning her, his big hard body showing her just how much he desired her.

Sophie shuddered with pleasure, but also need. She craved him, all of him, not just his body, but Joe, the man. She wanted to feel him and taste him and be one with him. Her feelings were strong, intense, overwhelming. She couldn't remember feeling this much for anyone before. Certainly not Leo.

Joe swept her into his arms and carried her to bed. Sophie unbuttoned his shirt and pushed the soft fabric from his shoulders, desperate to feel his skin against hers.

He kissed her as he stripped her, and kissed her as he stroked her, making her body tingle from head to toe. She arched against him, unsatisfied by the light touches and the kisses. Joe was her husband. She wanted to belong to him. It was time to have no more distance between them.

The driving need to be his only intensified when he filled her. His body on hers, his skin covering her, made her feel completely alive. Joe made love to her slowly, savoring the moment, extending the pleasure until she was panting and clinging to him, desperate for release. The climax shattered her, the orgasm so powerful it broke some little wall she'd had up, and she cried, and once she started crying she couldn't stop.

It wasn't that the sex wasn't good, it was the opposite.

Making love to Joe had been unlike anything she'd ever felt before. She felt real and known. Beautiful and valuable. His care for her had been evident in every caress, and every kiss, and in the way he'd made sure her need was met.

The closeness she felt was unlike anything she'd experienced with Leo. In Joe's arms, she finally felt peace.

Love.

In Joe's arms, she felt the meaning of love.

And so she cried, because she knew now that what she'd had with Leo had been empty, and she'd been too naïve to know, too silly and optimistic to understand that Leo hadn't cared for her. Leo had never made her feel this good, or this special, not even once.

She cried because maybe Sarah had been partially right. Maybe Sophie had gone through the motions, wanting a relationship, wanting to be part of a couple, and Leo had been convenient.

She cried because if this was how Leo felt with her sister Sarah, and Sarah felt with Leo, then they should be together. And they were right to end things.

And then Sophie cried because she'd been angry for months, angry with Sarah and Leo for betraying her, when really Sophie had betrayed herself, by settling for less, by being content with a relationship where she didn't matter, and hadn't ever truly mattered.

Joe held her through the tears and there were a lot of them.

"Why are you crying?" he asked when she finally grew quiet, his arm low around her waist, holding her securely to him.

"I realize I've made so many mistakes," she said, before hiccupping. "Too many. It's overwhelming."

"Want to talk about them?"

She shook her head. "No." She struggled to wipe her cheeks dry. "I'm too ashamed."

JOE HELD HER until she fell asleep, and then he eased away

and left the bed. He grabbed his jeans and boots and shirt carried them with him down the hall to the bathroom. It was the middle of the night but he took a shower, a long hot shower, before dressing and heading to the family room where he stretched out on the couch.

Making love to Sophie had been amazing, earth-shattering. Until she began to cry, and then once she started to cry, she couldn't stop and Joe realized that what had been powerful and life changing for him was a terrible mistake for her.

He slept for a few hours and then woke up before daybreak. In the kitchen, he splashed cold water on his face, made coffee, filled a thermos, and grabbed some day-old biscuits before heading to the barn. He had a lot of work to do, a long day in the saddle, and he had no idea when he'd be back.

Maybe because he didn't want to be back.

CHAPTER ELEVEN

SOPHIE HAD MONDAY off, which meant she was home all day waiting for Joe to appear, but he didn't return to the house for lunch, and he wasn't back late afternoon, either.

He never stayed out after dark.

The long-standing rule for all ranch employees was that everybody reported in before dusk. In all the time Sophie had known Joe, he'd never been late, he'd never not returned by dark. He was like clockwork. Four thirty, he was in. Four thirty, his horse was groomed, animals fed, he was in the kitchen washing up to help with dinner, or assist his mom.

But it was most definitely dark now and Joe wasn't back.

Her heart hurt, and her eyes burned and she paced the kitchen frantically, watching the clock, waiting for his boots to thud on the porch before he'd open that back door.

Fifteen minutes passed, and then a half hour, but still no sign of Joe.

Finally, heartsick, she started dinner, browning the pork chops even as she swung from fear to anger and back to fear again. She was worried. Had something happened to him? Why hadn't he come back? Why did no one else seem bothered by the fact that Joe wasn't home?

She headed for the family room where Granddad and Summer were watching the evening news.

"Dinner's almost ready," she said.

"Should we eat in here tonight?" Melvin said. "We can eat as we watch the news."

"Joe's not back yet," Sophie said, feeling as if they knew something she didn't know, because they never ate in front of the TV and it was almost an hour past the time they normally ate. "Joe hasn't returned yet, and that's not like him."

Melvin muted the TV. "He's back," he said bluntly. "He's fine."

Sophie's heart lifted, and relief swept through her. She almost felt dizzy at the news. "I didn't see him come in. When did he get back?"

"You probably won't see him tonight," Summer said. "He's sleeping in the bunkhouse tonight."

Sophie froze. "Why?" she asked, before she could stop herself.

There was an uncomfortable beat of silence for a moment, and then Melvin said, "Joe just needs some time. Even as a boy, if he got upset, he needed space and time."

Sophie slowly understood what they were saying, what was happening. "He doesn't want to see me."

"Just give him time," Summer said with a sympathetic smile. "I know it's not easy, but everything will work out."

SUMMER WAS RIGHT about one thing; it wasn't easy giving Joe time. His silence felt like rejection, and the rejection felt like abandonment. Sophie wasn't ready for this. She didn't feel strong enough. She wasn't prepared.

She suddenly felt like it was December and her entire world was crashing in again. It hadn't crossed her mind that Leo would leave her. And now Joe didn't want to see her. He didn't want to talk to her. He wanted nothing to do with her. And Sophie didn't know what to do. She felt absolutely desperate, and cried herself to sleep, only to waken an hour later, numb and heartsick.

Was it over between them?

Joe's mom had counseled for Sophie to be patient, and give Joe space, and time, but that was also the very thing Leo's mom had told her when he'd ended things.

He just needs time.

He'll come around.

But he didn't. And Sophie didn't think Joe would, either.

In the morning, after what had been an endless, sleepless night, Sophie started to cry yet again, and they were exhausted tears, but also furious tears because this wasn't the marriage she'd come to Montana for.

This wasn't the practical businesslike arrangement they'd wanted.

This was awful, and emotional, and heartbreaking, and

obviously Joe wanted no part of it, and to be honest, she didn't want it, either.

She wanted what they'd agreed to—practical.

Unemotional.

Safe.

Love wasn't safe. Love was intense and confusing and awful.

Crying, Sophie began to pack, shoving her clothes and shoes into her oversized suitcases. She didn't know where she would go. She didn't know what she was going to do. She did have work in a little less than two hours, and she debated calling in sick, but that didn't seem fair to Amanda, so no, she'd go to Marietta, and work, and then she'd try to figure out what she was going to do both in the short-term and the long-term.

Sophie carried her things downstairs, wondering if she bumped into in any of the Wyatt family, but the downstairs was quiet, most of the rooms dark. She suspected that Granddad was already out in the barn, and Summer must still be in bed. Summer tended to sleep in in the mornings, probably because she stayed up late each night.

She poured herself a cup of the coffee that had been made, doctored it so that it was the way she liked it, and shushing the dogs, carried her things out to the car. It required two trips, and then a third for her coffee mug.

She'd have to get the mug and the car back to Joe.

She'd have to get her heart back, too, but she didn't

know when that would happen.

Hot tears burned her eyes. She blinked hard, hating the lump filling her throat.

Sophie climbed behind the steering wheel and started the engine. She glanced up at the two-story log cabin house and saw a curtain move in the room on the far right. Summer's room.

Sophie's chest squeezed tightly. Had Summer seen her load the car with her things?

Fighting fresh tears, she reversed the small SUV even as she kept an eye on the dogs, and then she shifted into drive and accelerated, leaving the Wyatt ranch behind.

"YOU LOOK REALLY rough," Amanda said later that morning, as she stopped by the reception desk in the salon to say hello to Sophie.

"I feel pretty rough," Sophie admitted.

"Let me guess. First fight with Joe?"

And just like that the sting of tears returned. "Close. It's my last fight with Joe." Sophie's voice cracked. "I've left the ranch; have moved out of the Wyatt's house."

"Why?"

"I realized I can't do this… can't pretend I don't want more, or need more, when I do."

"So you're… done? You're just leaving him?"

Sophie squeezed her eyes shut, but even then, she could

see Joe, and feel him, and feel how much she loved him. She didn't want to leave him, and she couldn't imagine being without him now. In six weeks, his world had become her world, and his family had become her family, and she'd come to love Montana.

And Joe.

How she loved Joe.

"I don't know what I'm going to do," Sophie confessed. "I just… I'm… hurt. Really hurt, and really angry. And most of all, confused. I never thought he'd do this."

"What did he do?"

"He disappeared. He just… left, moving into the bunkhouse. I don't understand. Why would he just shut me out?"

"That's not like Joe. Something must have happened."

"We made love and then he disappeared."

"Okay, something happened. What happened?"

Sophie's eyes filled with tears. "I cried after."

"You cried, sometimes women do that after sex."

"But I didn't stop crying for a long time."

"Oh."

Sophie nodded and chewed on the inside of her lip. "I need to talk to him."

"I agree, but don't you think that's a conversation you should have with him face-to-face?"

"Yes." Sophie rubbed beneath her eyes. "I hate that I packed my things. I hate that I left."

"No one knows you left. He probably doesn't know

you've left yet. Go home and talk to him. It might be hard but isn't he worth it?"

"Absolutely."

Amanda glanced at her watch. "Do you want to leave now? We can manage without you. We survived for a week without a receptionist before you started."

"I'm not ready to go back yet. I think having a little break is good for me, but what if I head back after lunch? So I'll stick around and work half day?"

"Sounds good, but if you need to leave sooner, you can."

Sophie was busy restocking shampoos and conditioners and styling products into the glass display when she glanced out the front window and spotted a familiar person slowly heading up the sidewalk to the salon's front door.

Joe's mom was here.

Sophie froze for a moment before she came back to life, rushing to the door to open it for her mother-in-law. "What are you doing here? Do you have an appointment?" Sophie asked, feeling stupid and confused all over again.

"No. I just came to see you."

"Did Granddad bring you?"

"No."

"Joe?"

"No."

A lump filled Sophie's throat and she swallowed hard. "How did you get here then?"

"I borrowed Joe's truck."

Sophie suddenly felt faint. "You're joking."

"It was the only vehicle available." She grimaced. "It was very difficult getting into it, and I almost fell getting out of it, but no matter. I'm here. I didn't die, although driving, there was a moment where I swerved and almost hit a tree—"

"Summer, you're terrifying me."

"Me as well. It's not that easy of a truck to drive."

"No, I guess not." Sophie took her by the elbow. "Should we go sit down? Would you like a cup of coffee, or tea? There might be some bubbly water in the refrigerator."

"I would like to sit and rest."

"I think we both should sit. I'm about to have a heart attack just listening to your adventures getting here." She walked Joe's mom down the small hall and out the back to a small covered porch filled with white wicker furniture and pink and green pillows. "I'll get us some water, and I'll be right back."

Sophie grabbed her phone, sent Joe a text. "*Your mom is here in Marietta. She came in your truck.*" And then she took two bottles of chilled water from the refrigerator and hurried out to the porch where Summer was waiting for her in a wicker rocking chair.

Sophie removed the lid from one water and handed it to her mother-in-law.

"Isn't this delightful?" Summer said, her gaze sweeping the porch and the little garden beyond. "So pretty and feminine. I didn't get the appeal of a pink salon but I might be changing my mind."

Sophie sat down across from her and leaned forward. "Summer, does anyone know you're here?"

"No."

"So you just took Joe's truck and came here?" Sophie didn't mean for her voice to rise but she felt beyond panicked and anxious. Hopefully Joe would see her text soon. He didn't want everyone worried, and they would worry when they discovered Summer gone.

"Yes."

"Why?"

"I needed to talk to you, and no, it wasn't convenient getting here, but I'm here, and I won't have him interfering. Men can be useless, and clueless, and Joe is no exception."

Sophie didn't know if she felt better or worse. "Maybe we should call, tell Granddad."

"They're both out on their horses, riding in the back-country. I'll be back before he even notices that either of us are gone," she said, emphasizing the last words, even as her gaze met Sophie's and held. Most pointedly.

Sophie's heart fell. So Summer had seen her carry all her bags out to the Jeep. And now she was here, despite driving being painful for her.

Sophie rubbed at her forehead, the dull ache intensifying. "It's not what it looks like," she said. "All my bags in the car."

"I'm not here to tell you what to do, Sophie. I'm not

here to judge you, either. Marriage is hard, even when you're madly in love with the other person. I can't imagine how challenging it must be to marry a virtual stranger."

Sophie's head jerked up and her gaze met Summer's.

"I know more than you think I know," Summer admitted with a faint smile. "I know about the wife wanted ad on that agriculture dating website—"

"What?"

Summer nodded. "Billy told me. And then I found it, thanks to my iPad. I love my iPad."

Sophie's head was spinning. "So that first day when I arrived at the house… you knew?"

"I knew you'd come to Montana to marry my Joe, yes."

"You weren't happy."

"I didn't know you, and I was suspicious. What were your motives? Why would you give up your life in California to move to our ranch in Paradise Valley?" She paused, lips pursing. "And then you married at the courthouse just days later. I was not happy, but I was also intrigued."

Sophie's mouth dried. "How did you find that out?"

"My good friend Alice Watkinson works at the courthouse and spotted you two getting your marriage license, and then heading upstairs to the judge's office."

"So you've known all this time?"

"Yes."

"But you said nothing."

"I was interested in seeing how you two were going to make this work. You've surprised me. I didn't think an internet relationship would be successful, but you two have proved me wrong."

"So if you knew about the courthouse wedding, why are we doing this second wedding?"

"Because I wasn't there at the first, and none of my friends were there at the first. Dad wasn't there. Joe's brothers weren't there. We want to celebrate with you."

Sophie's eyes narrowed. She eyed her mother-in-law suspiciously, remembering Joe's words, *she's that smart.*

"Why do I feel like the wedding plans were a test?" Sophie said after a moment. "Because you weren't happy in the beginning. You were mad—"

"Not mad, but concerned. I had my doubts."

"So all those painful, uncomfortable wedding discussions…"

"They weren't all uncomfortable," Summer answered with a faint smile.

"Most of them were. You were so…" Sophie struggled to find the right word. "Difficult. And stubborn. You wanted what you wanted."

"I did. You're absolutely right. I wanted my Joe happy. I wanted my son to marry someone who cared about him. I wanted my son to have a wife who put him first, because as much as I loved Charity, and I did adore Charity, she never put Joe first. She couldn't understand why the ranch was so important to him, and yet you, an outsider, got it right away. And you, Sophie Correia Wyatt, are the wife he deserves. You're exactly the wife I would want for him. Exactly the wife I'd pick if it were up to me. Strong, kind, independent, loving. You're the perfect wife for him, and once I realized that, I wanted you two to have a proper wedding. Because you deserve it. You both deserve all the happiness in the world."

❦

SOPHIE LEFT JOE'S truck in town, parked in front of the Wright Salon, and drove Summer back to the ranch in the hunter-green Jeep. Joe was standing in the middle of the circular driveway when they arrived home. He helped his mom out of the car, and saw her into the house before returning outside to join Sophie on the long covered porch.

"You came back," he said roughly.

There was a raw note of pain in his deep voice and it reached into her chest and made her heart knot and ache.

"I had to come back," she said. "Your mom needed a ride." Then she added, "And because I made a promise to you that if I leave, I'll always come back. We're supposed to be a team." Her voice cracked and she felt so bruised on the inside. "And let's be honest, Joe. You were the one that left me."

"I didn't leave you. I was simply giving you space."

"But you moved out into the bunkhouse. You didn't talk to me. You did everything you could to avoid me. You effectively shut me out, ignoring me as if I no longer existed."

"I thought you might need it."

"Why would I want to feel rejected and abandoned?"

"I didn't reject you," he growled. "That's not what happened."

"No? What happened then?"

"We made love and you regretted it—"

"I didn't regret it."

"You cried."

"Because the orgasm was intense."

"You cried for a very long time, Sophie."

"I know, and I'm sorry if it made you feel weird. I was just overwhelmed."

"That's why I left. I wasn't punishing you. I was trying to give you space, and privacy—" He broke off before he finished tightly, "I know you still have feelings for Leo and I'm beginning to realize you have regrets—"

"Oh, Joe, you've got it all wrong. I don't love Leo. I don't love him anymore, at all. Did he hurt me? Yes. He betrayed me, and broke my trust, but I don't love him, or miss him, or want to be with him."

"You cried after we made love."

"I cried because the sex we had, you and me, was so good. I cried because it felt so right. I cried because I realized what I once felt for Leo was nothing compared to what I feel for you." She grabbed him by the shirt and gave it a fierce shake. "Being with you, making love with you, made me realize how lucky I am to have found you—"

He interrupted her words, silencing them with a kiss.

The kiss went on and on, and she clung to him, thinking no one and nothing had ever felt better.

When he finally lifted his head, she smiled a watery smile up at him. "I love you. Madly in love with you, Joe, and terrified you will stop wanting me—"

"No, never. Ever. Sophie, I love you."

Her skin prickled all over. Her hair rose on her nape. "Did you just say…"

"Yes. I love you, and I think I fell in love with you the moment you stepped off that plane and walked into the terminal with your long gorgeous hair and those polarized sunglasses. You looked like a movie star and then you took your glasses off and I saw you'd been crying and all I've wanted since that day was to take care of you. I want a life with you, a big life, a happy life. I want everything with you."

"Say it again," she whispered.

"I love you and want everything with you."

"And again."

"I love you—"

"Once more."

"I love you."

"Thank God." She smiled even as tears fell. "And I love you, Joe Wyatt, with all of my heart and all of my soul."

Then he kissed her, deeply, passionately, and Sophie's bruised heart healed, and her world was complete.

EPILOGUE

S UNDAY ARRIVED WITH a breathtaking rose-and-gold sunrise, the brilliant rays casting a peach glow over Paradise Valley. The wedding wouldn't be for hours yet, but Sophie lingered with her coffee at the window in Joe's room, which, as of today, was officially her room, too. Joe had helped her clear her things out of Sam's room and move her into his room, even as he apologized for not having a bigger, nicer bedroom. She didn't care about the size of the room; the bed was big and comfortable, topped with a fluffy feather duvet.

She'd been secretly sleeping in here every night since she and Joe had made up—not that it was probably a secret to the rest of the household. But no one said anything and Sophie was just so happy to finally be totally comfortable here at the ranch house. She didn't ever want to have another big fight with Joe. It had been horrible, and scary, and incredibly sad, but the fight—and the aftermath—had changed something in them. It'd changed their relationship, too. They felt like a real couple, and their relationship felt solid, and safe.

In the future, she expected they'd have arguments and would lose their tempers, but there would be no walking out, or running away. There would be no extended periods of silence or hurtful distancing. They'd both agreed they would never again go to bed angry with the other. They'd promised to talk more, and work on communication. But, honestly, communication had changed tremendously already. Just being together in the same bed at night made communication easy. Joe had dropped the last of his guard and he smiled so much more, even his expression when he looked at Sophie made her heart melt. His lovely blue eyes warmed when he looked her way, his expression so full of tenderness and love that it made her feel breathless. No one had ever looked at her this way, or made her feel so special, as if she was something miraculous.

She loved the laughter in the house now, too. Granddad was exactly as he'd always been—strong, quiet, but loving. It was Summer who'd changed. She was happy, and so light-hearted, she struck Sophie as almost girlish. Joe still wasn't pleased that his mom had deliberately been cold to Sophie, but Sophie understood.

"Don't be upset with her," Sophie said last night, snuggling against his chest. "She wanted what was best for you, and you got it… me!"

He laughed, the sound a warm rumble, and his arms tightened around her and he dropped a kiss on the top of her head. "Tomorrow we have wedding number two. Are you really good with it, or have you just become an exceptional actress?"

"I'm actually really excited. I never did have a wedding. I had an engagement. But I never did wear a pretty dress, or walk down an aisle, or have a first dance or cut a cake." She fell silent a moment, picturing everything that would happen tomorrow. "Even if no one comes, it will be special just being with you, celebrating us."

And now here it was, the big day, and Sophie felt another jolt of excitement as she heard and then saw a big white truck come into view. The dogs dashed out into the driveway, beyond excited, with Runt practically doing backflips in his eagerness to get to the passengers.

Joe's brothers had arrived.

And then Joe was stepping out of the house, heading to the driveway and she watched as the truck doors opened and three big cowboys climbed out and then Joe was hugging them, and they were back-slapping and laughing, and hugging some more.

Sophie's eyes filled with tears, but they were happy tears.

Joe had been so lonely here with them gone. He'd been so lonely at the ranch before she arrived, and now he never had to be the oldest, doing the responsible thing, alone. She'd be at his side, supporting him, and caring for him, and instead of being practical and businesslike, they'd fill this old ranch house full of love and laughter. And babies. Hopefully at least four or five.

Suddenly, all the guys outside were looking up to the window where she stood and they waved. She waved back and then she quickly wiped away a tear. She was happy. She loved it here. She felt as if she'd truly come home.

❦

SOPHIE WAS IN her dressing room at Emerson Barn getting ready. The wedding was just an hour away now, and Amanda had arrived to do Sophie's hair and makeup. Summer knocked at the door, asking if she could come in, and Sophie had welcomed her. "I'm glad you're here," Sophie said. "It makes it more special."

Summer carefully sat in one of the chairs by the window. She looked almost radiant in her cream gown with the antique lace overlay. Amanda had done Summer's hair earlier, and her silvery-blonde style flattered her immensely.

Summer couldn't help beaming as she watched Amanda curl Sophie's hair. "I have to tell you, Sophie, I haven't had this much fun in ages. Thank you so much for indulging me. I know you didn't want to do all of this—"

"In the beginning," Sophie agreed, "but I'm glad you insisted we have a wedding. This is wonderful, it is."

"Well, I appreciate you including me, and letting me help create a dream wedding for you and Joe. I just want you two to know how much we love you."

"I do know." Sophie's gaze met Summer's in the mirror. "How does it feel, having all your boys home?"

"Wonderful. They have so much fun together. The photographer, McKenna Sheenan, is with them now, taking pictures. She'll be coming here soon to take pictures of you in your dress."

"I don't think I've met her yet."

"She grew up in this valley. Her family were ranchers, too."

Amanda leaned down and whispered into Sophie's ear, "McKenna's brother, Quinn, is the baseball player that married Charity."

Sophie was almost finished dressing when the photographer arrived. McKenna quickly set up lights and began taking candids of Summer straightening Sophie's veil, and Amanda touching up Sophie's makeup.

And then it was time to go and Sophie's heart beat faster.

JOE HAD BEEN standing with the minister, waiting for Sophie to arrive. The guests filled the folding chairs and his mother had been seated five minutes earlier, walked to her chair up front by Sam. Joe had given her a wink as she sat down and she gave him a proud smile. This day meant so much to her. She'd made that promise to Joe's dad to do her best for the boys, and she had. Today, her eldest was getting married.

Turning his head, Joe glanced at his brothers who stood by his side, quietly joking and talking. Joe had known they were driving through the night to make the wedding, but seeing Sam's truck this morning pull into the driveway, and then having them spill out of the truck, boisterous and happy to be home, had given him peace. Everyone told him that his brothers looked a lot like him, and he supposed they did. The Wyatts inherited Melvin's height, and lean, athletic build. His brothers were also tan and tough, hardened by competition, and weathered by competing in all elements.

Joe's gaze met Sam's, and Sam grinned. Joe grinned back. Smiled. Even though he was no longer on the road with Sam, Billy, and Tommy, they were still close, and he knew they'd be here today. He would have bet the ranch on it.

Suddenly, the music changed and the familiar strains of the bridal march played. Joe looked up, and there was Sophie, entering the big barn on his grandfather's arm.

His heart kind of stopped.

He, who never cried, felt his eyes sting. Joe blinked hard to see her better.

She wasn't wearing white. She wore a light blue gown with a delicate lace bodice with a frothy tulle skirt that floated around her, making her look like a cloud as she walked down the aisle on Granddad's arm. Her long hair had been curled and styled, and she carried a bouquet of white roses and lilies. She finally had the flowers she deserved. She was so beautiful, perfect in every way.

She smiled at him as she approached, and for a second, Joe couldn't breathe. It was impossible when his chest ached, his heart full.

He'd placed an ad for a wife, and God had sent him an angel.

THE END

The Wyatt Brothers of Montana series

Book 1: *Montana Cowboy Romance*

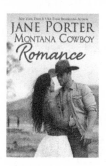

Book 2: *Montana Cowboy Christmas*
Pre-order now!

Book 3: *Montana Cowboy Daddy*
Coming soon!

MORE BY JANE PORTER

Love on Chance Avenue series

Book 1: *Take Me, Cowboy*
Winner of the RITA® Award for Best Romance Novella

Book 2: *Miracle on Chance Avenue*

Book 3: *Take a Chance on Me*

Book 4: *Not Christmas Without You*

Available now at your favorite online retailer!

The Taming of the Sheenans series

The Sheenans are six powerful wealthy brothers from Marietta, Montana. They are big, tough, rugged men, and as different as the Montana landscape.

Christmas at Copper Mountain
Book 1: Brock Sheenan's story

Tycoon's Kiss
Book 2: Troy Sheenan's story

The Kidnapped Christmas Bride
Book 3: Trey Sheenan's story

Taming of the Bachelor
Book 4: Dillion Sheenan's story

A Christmas Miracle for Daisy
Book 5: Cormac Sheenan's story

The Lost Sheenan's Bride
Book 6: Shane Sheenan's story

Available now at your favorite online retailer!

ABOUT THE AUTHOR

New York Times and USA Today bestselling author of over fifty five romances and women's fiction titles, **Jane Porter** has been a finalist for the prestigious RITA award five times and won in 2014 for Best Novella with her story, Take Me, Cowboy, from Tule Publishing. Today, Jane has over 12 million copies in print, including her wildly successful, Flirting With Forty, picked by Redbook as its Red Hot Summer Read, and reprinted six times in seven weeks before being made into a Lifetime movie starring Heather Locklear. A mother of three sons, Jane holds an MA in Writing from the University of San Francisco and makes her home in sunny San Clemente, CA with her surfer husband and two dogs.

Thank you for reading

Montana Cowboy Romance

If you enjoyed this book, you can find more from all our great authors at TulePublishing.com, or from your favorite online retailer.

TULE
PUBLISHING

Made in the USA
Coppell, TX
10 September 2021

62142635R00156